'Lucky' Montana

Sean Rafferty only wanted enough money to buy back the ruins of his family's estate in Ireland. Trouble was, he didn't care how he got his hands on that money or how many lives he ruined in the process.

The man they called 'Lucky' Montana found that fate threw him into the deal. With a bounty hunter already stalking him, Montana now had to contend with Rafferty's murderous crew as well.

Now he must stride into battle, with the knowledge that there is always a quick bullet waiting for him.

'Lucky' Montana

CLAYTON NASH

A Black Horse Western

ROBERT HALE · LONDON

© Clayton Nash 2005
First published in Great Britain 2005

ISBN 0 7090 7770 X

Robert Hale Limited
Clerkenwell House
Clerkenwell Green
London EC1R 0HT

Typeset by
Derek Doyle & Associates, Shaw Heath.
Printed and bound in Great Britain by
Antony Rowe Limited, Wiltshire

CHAPTER 1

ALL KINDS
OF LUCK

He had often thought that the fool who had tagged him with the nickname of 'Lucky' – a tinhorn named Cash O'Brien – ought to be damn well shot.

This was another of those times.

O'Brien hadn't been shot but someone had slipped a knife between his ribs in a steamy rat-hole of a southern prison. That day he had almost wept – not because O'Brien had died, but because he hadn't been the one to send him to that big Poker Game in the sky.

Now none of it mattered.

'Lucky' was once again about to be proved a misnomer . . .

He could hear them on the stairs, coming up like treacle leaking from a cracked jug. There had been a muffled thud on the balcony outside the room, too.

He swore softly: he had come in here too damn fast after he had recognized Dawson down on Main, picked the wrong room. The room he really wanted was next door. It had a balcony, but a short private one, separate to the long one that ran alongside the north-eastern wall of the hotel. Now it was too late to change.

Or was it?

If he stayed here he was a goner. They'd get him in a crossfire, blasting in the door while others poured hot lead in from the balcony window. *OK!*

That left only one thing to do: make a run for the room next door and hope like hell it wasn't occupied.

But first he had to get out of his door and make a run along the hallway to the room he wanted. He had noticed earlier it was entirely separate to this part of the hallway, the door a little more ornate, twenty feet away at least.

Jesus, it might be a suite of rooms, full of people!

Only one way to find out, and without hesitation he unshipped his six-gun, took the spare from his warbag – he'd have to abandon that – and went to the door. An ear against the cold wood of the panel told him they were halfway up the stairs already – he had taken note of that creaky step when he had arrived. So he couldn't delay any longer.

And he didn't.

He wrenched open the door and went out shooting, left-hand gun blazing for the wild shots that would scatter the armed men on the stairs – *he hoped!* – keeping the right-hand Colt for the more serious business of bringing down the most dangerous of the posse.

His gunfire caused chaos on the stairs. Bullets whistled and splintered the wall and banister rails. Men yelled, the foremost trying to turn back, running into those behind who were still swarming upwards. There was a tangle and much cussing, a couple of men slipping and others falling over them. One man tumbled over the rail and landed on the floor like a spread crucifix, his back obviously damaged.

A lanky man broke through the mess, stumbling as he walked over the writhing bodies of his companions as he brought up his Greener and loosed off a charge of double-o buckshot. It chewed a good portion out of the rails edging the landing as the fugitive made his crouching run down the hallway, left hand thrust behind, firing his last shots in that six-gun. He ducked, slipped, skidded on the polished linoleum. He travelled faster this way and was down low so that the second charge of buckshot punched a large ragged hole in the wall three feet above his head.

He rolled and lunged for the ornate doorway, turning his left shoulder into the carved panel. The door trembled, but held, shrugged off his efforts. He sucked in a ragged breath as he found his balance and placed a boot violently over the lock area. Wood splintered and the nicely polished brass plate buckled as it tore out of the woodwork.

He was moving in a stumbling run when he entered, heard someone scream and glimpsed four

7

people standing wide-eyed by a candle-lit table obviously set for supper, half-eaten food on the hotel's best plates.

Damn! It was *a suite of rooms!*

But the well-dressed, well-fed folk were too stunned or afraid to make any kind of a move to stop him. There were roars of vengeance out in the passage, the thud of booted feet coming. He rammed his empty gun into his belt, waved the other Colt vaguely at the group, then scooped up an occasional table that held a tall vase of flowers and decorative prairie grass. But not for long. It toppled and shattered and by that time he was moving like a log in a waterslide, table lowered at the french doors with their drawn drapes.

They yielded to the power of his charge, the table almost jarring from his grip as it smashed the doors open, glass tinkling. He had time to groan once when he saw he was on the small balcony but then he hit the rail and the table splintered in his hand.

So did the rail.

His yell made a brief fading wail as he sailed out into the night high above Main and its traffic of wagons and riders and people.

But it was only a fleeting glimpse as he dropped like a stone off a cliff. Something high and black and looking as solid as a mountain rushed to meet him and he thought, *Lucky? Hell, I wish I'd killed that son of a . . .*

He hit. It was hard, but not as hard as he expected. Breath slammed from his lungs and every bone and joint in him jarred agonizingly. He tasted salt and his

8

eyes stung, there was a crackling of something – and then he *bounced*!

His yell was tremulous as his body lifted a couple of feet in the air and he was flung, tumbling, down the high side of a slab-bodied wagon and a foul stench filled his nostrils, constricted his throat. Even as he floundered onto the muddy street he realized he had fallen onto a buffalo-runner's hide wagon. It was packed with tightly rolled, salted hides with a couple of unsalted, partly fleshed skins on top to keep off the dirt and the frost that had laid a thin layer of ice on them.

That had made the crackling sound as he hit. Then he splashed into the mud again and lost some more breath that he couldn't afford, skidding and rolling. A couple of riders flanking the wagon cursed him and hauled their mounts aside. He ploughed through the slush, found he was sliding between the wheels of a second wagon, ducked his head and slid on through. By that time he had some kind of control and managed to slow, slew around on his belly, spitting mud, gagging.

Blinking his vision clear, he coughed up some muck and thrust to hands and knees, surprised to find he still held his six-gun.

'Man, you got the luck of the devil hisself!' opined a rider, hauling rein and leaning from the saddle to offer his hand.

Then there were shouts from the hotel balcony, men calling for riders and wagon drivers to clear the street, to get the hell out of the way. Someone fired into the air to give weight to the warning and the fugitive took the hand of the helpful rider, hauled to his feet – and promptly yanked the man out of the saddle.

The cowboy yelled and splashed into the mud.

Guns hammered above as the armed men saw what their quarry was about. Men scattered, drivers tried to whip their ponderous wagons out of the way, a woman screamed, horses whinnied and whirled and reared, cannoned into one another.

Through the middle of all this unscheduled entertainment on Main, the lucky fugitive lay along the neck of his newly acquired mount and spurred into the cold night.

Lucky? Hell, maybe Cash O'Brien knew what he was talking about after all.

They got him on the very first day of spring, riding casually into a town called Murphy Creek at the base of the Rockies where they spurred eastward south of Cheyenne.

He was heading south, going to meet the warmer weather, his bones still aching from the long winter up north. Strangely enough, he was still riding the horse he had taken off the helpful cowboy back in Rapid City in the Black Hills of Dakota.

It was a good, range-bred smoke with a distinctive dark, saddle-patch under the left eye. He had rubbed light-coloured clay into this often, gradually covering it, although a shadow was still noticeable. *Just in case.* . . .

And the thing was, this keen-eyed lawman just stopping over in Murphy Creek after checking out a

10

bunch of rustlers to the west, spotted the damn horse! Turned out he was a range detective, employed by a Cattlemen's Association in Casper, Wyoming, on his way home, decided to visit with his son and his family in Murphy before heading west.

And he had been in the livery, passing the time of day with the liveryman, who turned out to be the detective's son. As the smoke had been backed into a stall and unsaddled, the lawman sauntered in, leaned a shoulder against a post and lit his pipe, which he smoked left-handed. He gestured to the horse's head with the charred bowl.

'Fine-looking bronc – don't see many like him this far north.'

He earned a grunt from the rider as he swung the saddle across the stall partition. The man's son, apparently recognizing something in his father's voice, paused as he made to move away, casually picked a long-handled pitchfork off the wall – and waited.

'What happened to his eye?'

'Nothing . . . that's just dirt. I'll get rid of it when I curry-comb him. '

The newcomer frowned as the lawman – he suspected he was *some* kind of sticky-nosed law – walked slowly around the smoke, gentling it with a lightly placed hand, pipe now clenched between his teeth.

'This here hoss belongs to the Casper Creek Cattlemen's Association that I work for. Name's Enright. I got a list of riders that work for 'em. Now, your name'd be . . . ?'

11

What was the use? His luck had held all through winter. Well, almost. There was that second run-in with Dawson but that could yet turn out to be good luck. Still, it was time for it to run bad again and he was too damn weary and hungry to care.

'I bought this gelding up in Dakota. '

'Rapid City by any chance?'

The son of a bitch knew! His luck had turned all right, turned right around and spat in his eye!

'No – Deadwood.'

Enright smiled thinly. 'I think Rapid City. That's as far as I trailed a rustler I was chasin', feller name of Brady. Still ain't heard your name, son. '

'Montana,' the trapped rider said with a heavy sigh.

'Got a monicker to go with that?'

He hesitated, then, 'They call me "Lucky" – God knows why!'

Enright and his son both grinned. 'Someone had a sense of humour!' allowed the son, chuckling.

'A real first name,' insisted the detective and Montana shrugged.

'Got lost somewhere in between "Lucky" and "Montana", long time ago. . . .'

'Uh-huh. Well, I reckon I could find a dodger out on you, all right. But don't matter really – I got you for hoss-stealin' and the Association'll want a piece of your hide. '

He protested, of course, got nowhere, not with the twin, shiny tines of a pitchfork up against his chest and Enright's Colt pressed into his side as the man lifted his gun from his holster and rammed it into his own belt. The range detective was a hickory-lean man of about fifty, weathered and grey-haired with a close-clipped moustache framing his thin lips. He had a satisfied look about him, a man used to success, and Montana's heart sank.

'Another one to chalk up for you, Pa,' said the liveryman. 'You must be sockin' away a decent pile of cash with all them bonuses the Association pay you. '

'Retire in two more years – I'll go into partnership with you and we'll have the best livery-cum-black-smith's-and-saddlery this side of the Rockies. '

The son's eyes gleamed: obviously this was one of his dreams.

'Lucky' Montana didn't give a spit in hell. All he knew he was caught, *manacled*, and headed in a direction he didn't want to go – back into Wyoming.

There was no chance of escape from Enright. Montana knew of the man's reputation. He'd never seen the man before but just mention the name and most folk this far north knew who you were talking about. A relentless man who ran down his prey until he either brought him in or shot it out and carried just the ears back to his Association bosses.

The detective got the notion into his head that Montana was a member of this highly organized rustler gang he had been pursuing. So he treated him mighty roughly, actually beat him once. Then took it into his head that other members of the gang might try to bust Montana loose.

'You're crazy! I'm not a member of any gang! I'm a loner, a drifter, just heading south for some warmth and a riding job with any ranch that'll have me. '

'Wrong – you're headin' west, and the only ridin' you'll be doin' is through the air at the end of a rope with a hangman's noose under your left ear – after I collect my bounty on you.'

'Like I said, plumb loco!'

That earned him a kidney punch and Enright made arrangements for their passage on a nine-car freight headed in the direction of Casper.

It was a long, slow climb over the range and Montana had no sooner had the idle thought that the loco was going slow enough for anyone who felt like it to step on board and shove a gun in the engineer's face than the whole train suddenly shuddered to a halt, cars banging and clanging on the couplings, transferring the sudden cessation of movement clear down to the caboose where Enright and his prisoner travelled.

The train guard leaned far out, holding to a brass rail, looking along the still shuddering line of cars to where the locomotive had stopped, steam hissing, but not loud enough to drown the sound of gunshots from up there.

'Judas priest! It's a goddamn hold-up!' exclaimed the guard, pale-faced as he hauled himself back into the caboose.

Enright had his gun out, glanced from Montana to the guard. 'You carryin'. . . . ?'

The guard swallowed, looked uneasy, then nodded. 'Payroll for the mines – but no one coulda known! It's been—'

Enright rounded on Montana, prodded him

14

hard with the six-gun in the ribs, causing the prisoner to doubleup. 'Not a member of any gang, huh! They dunno about the payroll, but they know about *you!*'

'No one knows about me,' Montana gritted, his ribs sore. 'Because I'm a loner – I told you. . . .'

By then Enright had his shirt collar bunched up and he dragged the prisoner past the frightened guard who was trying to unlock a chained shotgun on the wall. Montana staggered out onto the platform and started to yell as he was pushed violently over the rail. It hit him at hip level and he jack-knifed and crashed to the cinders on the side away from the bandits who were making their way down to the caboose. *They knew about the payroll all right!*

But it would be no use pointing that out to Enright.

The detective was beside him now, dragging him to his feet, shoving him roughly through the brush. Behind, a shotgun roared and then six-guns crackled and Montana turned in time to see two men swarming into the caboose, another down on the ground with an arm blown off at the shoulder.

One of the robbers on the steps saw Enright shoving Montana into the brush and fired a couple of shots. The detective fired back and the man swayed, clutching his shoulder, and hurled himself into the caboose for cover.

Enright pushed and dragged the manacled Montana through the brush and suddenly they were on the edge of a cliff above a boiling green river, frothing white where it surged between and over rocks. Montana balked, almost falling, held by Enright.

'Christ! That must be seventy feet down!' He gasped as he turned to Enright. 'Now that you've managed to wound one of them, they'll come after us! Thanks a lot, you goddamned idiot!'

Enright hit him across the jaw with the gun barrel, whirled as guns cracked and bullets tore through the brush. Three men were coming, wearing bandannas over their lower faces, guns smoking in their hands. Enright swore and shook the dazed Montana.

'Your damn cronies! Well, let's see how "lucky" you are – Lucky Montana!'

Then he grabbed the prisoner's arm and jumped into space, dragging a shouting Montana after him.

CHAPTER 2

WHO'S LUCKY?

Gavin Leach cut through the narrow draw he knew about, the one that would take him to the top of a ridge that looked out across the shallow basin that eventually became the Carnaby Desert. It was fierce and had claimed many lives, and was named after the first man to cross it and live – though Sergeant Carnaby hadn't lived for long, not even long enough to know they had named a geographical feature after him.

Leach wasn't sure what brought him up here to the ridge, only that it was a good place to sit and think – and wonder at the extremities of this wild country. A desert out there that would boil a man's brains in his skull. Yet, over his shoulder, beyond the brush-smeared ridge, lay the rich and green Viper River Valley.

He was supposed to be just riding line for Angie but it was not only boring, he didn't care for the

17

chore because he was afraid he might run into some of Rafferty's men.

Gavin Leach was only just twenty and he was a comparative newcomer to the frontier lands. Angie Bancroft was his sister, his widowed sister, and when he had heard of her tragedy, the death of her husband, Walt, after losing her two children to the plague that had swept this part of the country, he ran away from the boarding-school in Denver and came to help her on the ranch.

She was a stubborn woman was Angie, and she refused to consider selling – even though Rafferty made a handsome offer – dug in her heels and said she aimed to make a go of the A-Bar-W spread, just as Walt had planned.

Gavin sensed there was something more behind it but she didn't elaborate, in fact, berated him for quitting school.

'Walt and I worked hard to give you a chance at a good education, Gav,' she told him with that fire in her eye he had known all his life – she had reared him after their parents had died in a Comanche attack back in north-west Texas. 'You owe us something. You go back to school. I can manage here. '

'How?' he had flared, stung by her reaction to his sudden appearance: he'd had visions of being greeted like a hero. 'You've only got Link and old Horsehoe, and he's not even a good cook!'

'I'll manage.'

Gavin threw up his hands. 'Stubborn as always! Sis, I've learned all I want to – I can talk properly, know my manners, can quote from the Bible and do sums that'd make an ordinary man's head spin. But I'm just not an indoor type, not interested in living in a city or even a big town. I *like* it out here and I *want* to help you. And I'm going to.'

It didn't end there, of course. There were plenty of arguments over the next couple of weeks. But one evening, after her usual visit to the little graveyard atop the low knoll facing north where Walt lay between Bessie and little Joel, she came to him with a softer look on her work-worn though mighty handsome face and placed a hand on his arm, gentle as a butterfly landing on a prairie flower. Her clear hazel eyes moved slowly across his face, which was slightly tight, expecting another argument.

'Gav, I appreciate you coming here. You're right, I guess. Walt and I wanted you to have an education and then for you to use it whatever way you wished. If helping me out is what you want to do – and that's something I admit I need – then it's OK with me.' She smiled. 'I'm kind of – desperate, see. . . ?'

There was a little more to it than that, more explanations, more hugs and so on – they embarrassed him some, but he endured them because it was now going his way and, anyhow, he really did want to help. He owed Angie plenty.

He'd been here three weeks now and he had to admit that it was becoming a bit boring. Still, he would stick it out. He knew she had little money, couldn't understand why she didn't take Rafferty's offer and move closer to civilization.

He knew *why* she wanted to stay on, but damned if he understood it, not when she was struggling so

19

hard. Link was virtually useless, a ranny a bit older than Gavin but hard-muscled and tight-lipped. He resented Gavin's presence and Gavin figured Link might've had some notion of gradually moving in on Angie and taking over, making a nice little safe and profitable niche for himself with the widow woman.

Gavin had put paid to any such ideas: leastways, he thought he had. He found Link in the back of the barn one day, stretched out on a bale of hay, smoking.

'Ought to go outside if you're gonna smoke. A spark's all it'll take to send this place up.'

Link turned his head slowly, his wedge-shaped face impassive, eyes hard as he deliberately drew in deep on his cigarette and flicked some ash off the end.

'Word of an expert, huh?'

'Word of a partner in A-Bar-W,' Gavin gritted.

Link sat up, eyes slitted so that he had an almost Oriental look for a few moments. 'That the way it's goin' to be, huh? Figured you were just here for a holiday.'

'You're the one taking the holiday, looks like to me. Now, why don't you put out that cigarette and get to mending that loft ladder before you stack the hay up there?'

Link stood, three inches taller than Gavin's five-ten, broader, gun-hung, a man of the West, facing this greenhorn just in from having his diapers changed at some sissy damn Eastern school. He dragged on the cigarette again – jumped when Gavin slapped it from his hand, his fingertips making Link snap his head back as the nails stung his mouth.

Gavin ground the cigarette into the floor with a boot, looking coldly at Link all the time.

'The ladder needs repairs – Angie told you to get it done, not lie around risking fire in the barn.'

There was a slight tremor in Gavin's voice but he kept his mouth shut tight and his gaze steady. Link gave him a raking look, a cold study, assessing the situation. It was plain Link wanted to smash a fist into Gavin's face and he was a little surprised that he didn't try.

Then Link's shoulders relaxed some and, still looking mighty dangerous – *deadly* was a better word – he nodded.

'OK. But you ain't gonna bother me none, green-horn. You might think you're king of the dungheap, but maybe that'll change sooner than you think.' He picked up the broken loft ladder and stood it against the wall, seeing the two broken rungs, glanced over his shoulder at Gavin. 'You think about that. . . .'

Gavin did and it bothered him because he couldn't figure out what Link meant. But he said nothing to Angie – she had enough to worry about, what with mounting bills and broken fences and stock wandering all over the range.

Now, looking out over the heat-shimmer of the basin, Gavin wondered why she was having so much trouble with the ranch. Not that there hadn't been trouble before Walt had died but it seemed to be getting worse, more of it, and . . .

He stood in the stirrups suddenly, squinting, holding a hand above his eyes to reduce the glare. He took his field-glasses from his saddle-bag and focused them on the blurred movement out there in the shimmer. Some animal, hurt, looked like, crawling and floundering.

'Judas priest! It's a man!'

He rammed the glasses back into the bags and lifted the reins, heels touching his chestnut's flanks. The horse didn't want to go down the slope, knowing what the desolate basin was like – hard on the hoofs, dust that scoured eyes and nostrils, worked irritatingly into the genital pouch, and parched the throat.

But it had been trained to obey and it did so and in ten minutes Gavin was kneeling beside the hurt man. He was a rawboned type, muscles hard and long and powerful. He had a big lump with a short gash in the middle of it on his left temple. Dried blood, caked with alkali and sand had trickled in snaky patterns across his high-cheekboned face. Gavin turned him onto his back and a moan escaped the cracked lips.

The man's shirt was ripped and Gavin saw the body bruises and raw scrapes. The left arm was purple from shoulder to mid-forearm with massive bruising. The corduroy trousers were torn, showing one cut and swollen knee.

'God knows what's happened to you, feller,' Gavin said, unscrewing the cap of his canteen and lifting the man's head. 'You look like a survivor from a buffalo stampede.'

Gavin splashed water over the man's face, washing it free of alkali and grit and dried blood. A swollen tongue licked at the tepid liquid as it trickled over his lips. He made soft, unintelligible sounds deep in his throat.

He opened his mouth and Gavin let a little water trickle in. 'Not too much all at once,' he said pushing away the battered hand that tried to hold the canteen against his mouth.

That was when Gavin noticed the bruising on the man's wide wrist. The skin was torn and raw and blue-black, encircling the wrist completely. When he looked, Gavin found the swollen left wrist was the same.

He sat back as the man coughed up a little of the water.

He might be a greenhorn, but he had worked part-time deputy for the sheriff in Denver one trail-drive season during his college vacation, and he recognized the marks of handcuffs when he saw them.

'Mister,' he murmured, 'just what the hell have you been up to?'

By the time he rode back to the ridge, the stranger had slipped from the horse twice before Gavin could grab him.

The youngster winced each time as the man sprawled limply, jarred by his impact with the ground, adding to his already extensive injuries.

Gavin stopped on a rock ledge that looked back towards the ranch and, if he turned left, to the north-west, he could see part of Rafferty's big spread, too. He lifted the inert stranger one more time, dragged him up to a patch of grass and stretched him out. He covered him with a blanket as the man was starting to shiver despite the heat of the day. *Shock*, Gavin guessed.

Leach decided to camp here overnight. Angie wouldn't be expecting him back, although he had planned to cut corners and return to the ranch house instead of following the A-Bar-W line completely. No, he would camp here, he had enough grub, and a warm jacket. The stranger could have his blankets. Then he would make a *travois* like the Indians who worked on the ranch one time before they'd sent him south to school and college, had taught him. Angie would take care of him: she knew about treating injured rannies way out here.

He built a shelter with piñon branches over the stranger, made his camp-fire near its entrance so the man could get some of the warmth, and cooked a meal.

Gavin smiled as he took a sip of the hot, aromatic coffee, allowed his mind to drift while he chewed on the tough beefsteak he had brought from the ranch. It was cooked indifferently but filled a man's belly and gave him strength. Angie's cold biscuits tasted fine after he fried them up in the meat's grease.

The stranger moved under the blanket, rolling his head, muttering. Once, just after Gavin had turned in and the stars were blazing in a moonless sky, he had sat up and said clearly, '*I've never been lucky at cards – nor anything else.*'

Then he fell back and snored for most of the hours for the rest of the night. . . .

Gavin woke after sun-up, the glare stirring him, for he wasn't naturally an early riser. He rolled out of his blanket, emptied his bladder over the edge of the rock and stoked up his fire.

He had coffee bubbling in the battered trail pot when he heard a sound behind him. Thinking it was the stranger, maybe coming round, he turned casually. . . .

Gavin tasted bile and his belly lurched as he saw three man standing to one side of the pine-bough shelter where the injured man still slept. They held rifles, not pointed at him – yet – but he knew they would be soon.

'You're camped on Rafferty land here, kid,' said the man who stood slightly forward of the other two. He was solid as a mesa, shirt stretched tightly across heavy shoulders, the carbine like a toy in his large hands. He had a moon face, thick-lipped, heavy-browed, with tight-set eyes of a blue that reminded Leach of ice on a mountain stream.

'I'm not – this is Bancroft land!' Gavin knew he protested too loudly and his voice wasn't as steady as he wanted but his heart was hammering and he hoped his knees wouldn't shake noticeably.

'Sure of that, are you?' asked the big man. Gavin had never seen him before but he knew from Angie's description that he must be Claiborne, Rafferty's hardcase ramrod. The other two were Rafferty riders, McColl and Lindsey: he'd seen them in town once or twice and Angie had pointed them out to him.

'Yes – I'm sure!'

Claiborne smiled thinly, squinting. 'You'd be Angie's kid brother, huh? Come to protect her, I hear.'

Gavin swallowed, eyes flicking to where his own rifle rested beside his scattered bedroll, half-covered by the canvas outer layer.

'I-I came to lend my assistance on the ranch after Walt died. I – didn't expect she might need – protecting.'

Claiborne, clearly amused, looked around at the other two. 'Speaks fancy, don't he? Well, kid, I dunno whether Angie needs protectin' or not but I do know, if she does, you ain't the one to do it.' He jerked his head at the bough shelter. 'Nor that drifter you drug in from the edge of the desert.'

Gavin blinked. 'He's nothing to do with it! I just found him hurt. I was taking him in to get – looked after.'

'Yeah, he looked poorly when we seen him yest'y.'

The kid frowned. 'You *saw* him? Yesterday? And you didn't even try to help him?'

Claiborne shrugged. 'Just watched him through the glasses. Didn't look as if he'd make it. Wasn't no sense in wastin' time or messin' up our hosses' hoofs ridin' out to see.'

'But – but that – that's unforgivable! I thought you westerners were supposed to help *anyone* in trouble!'

'Ah, you been readin' too many dime novels, kid. Look, tell you what, you seem to be outa your depth here. This ain't really your style, ridin' range, is it?'

The man expected an answer so Gavin murmured, no, it wasn't, but he owed his sister and he wanted to help her. . . .

'Yeah, fine. You got a heart. Right – well, the best way you can help her is to tell her to take Mr

Rafferty's offer. It's a damn good one and was me, I'd take it quick as I could snap my fingers.'

Gavin Leach was sure his knees were shaking now and they surely must see them, but he swallowed, licked his dry lips and had to clear his throat before he said, 'She doesn't want to sell.'

Claiborne sighed, leaned forward, thrusting his heavy face towards the kid. 'Hell, we know that, for Chris'sake! What the hell is wrong with her? She wouldn't get another offer to top Mr Rafferty's!' He reached out suddenly and grabbed the front of Gavin's shirt and shook the startled youngster. 'I asked you a question! *What the hell is wrong with her?*'

'I-I don't know!' Gavin tried to open the big hand that gripped his clothes but the fingers were like steel clamps. 'It's her business. Let – me – go!'

'Aw, you hear that, boys? He wants me to let him go.' Claiborne started to drag the struggling kid towards the edge of the rock. 'Mebbe I'll do just that – but just a *leetle* closer to the edge, eh?'

'Hope he can fly, Clay!' chuckled McColl and Lindsey laughed out loud.

Gavin kicked at Claiborne's shins, startling the man and hurting him. The ramrod swore and shook Leach violently, backhanded him across the face.

'You little snake! I'm gonna beat your ribs around your goddamn backbone for that!' Without turning, he spoke to the advancing cowboys. 'Mac, you and Lin take hold this sonuver's arms while I give him a message for his sister. That's if she ain't too dumb to savvy it. . . .'

Gavin reacted instinctively, just as Claiborne

27

wanted him to. He tried to struggle free of the grip of McColl and Lindsey and, when he couldn't, spat at the ramrod, fouling the man's shirt.

'Ooh, now you gone an' done it, kid!' Lindsey said, winking at McColl. 'Bucktooth Bonnie give him that shirt for his birthday.'

Claiborne's fist was already working, slamming into Gavin's face, then his chest and his belly. He jack-knifed and Claiborne yelled to hold him up, set his boots solidly, shoulders spreading, preparing to give Gavin Leach the biggest hammering of his life.

Then there was a grunting sound and a *swish!* and suddenly a length of sapling that Gavin had cut last night to use on the *travois* smashed across Claiborne's head and knocked his hat spinning, driving the man to his knees. The sapling thudded again just where his neck joined his shoulders and he sprawled face down, one arm dangling over the edge of the rock. McColl and Lindsey let Gavin fall to his knees and reached for their six-guns.

The stranger stepped forward on unsteady feet and swung the sapling into Lindsey's midriff. The man gagged and retched as he collapsed, writhing. The sapling swung backhanded as McColl freed his six-gun from his holster and took him squarely across the face, smashing his nose, mouth and several teeth. McColl dropped, squirming and choking.

Breathing hard, the stranger leaned heavily on the sapling, blinking at Gavin, who, pale and startled, looked up at him from his hands and knees.

'You – you've killed them!' he gasped.

'No – not their – kind . . . Big drop off here?'

28

Gavin blinked again and shook his head. 'Six feet or so down to the next ledge.'

The stranger hobbled forward, kicked all three injured men over the edge of the rock. They hit awkwardly and sprawled amongst the brush and tufty grass and rocks six feet below.

'Find their hosses and run 'em off – they can walk back. If they're able.'

The stranger seemed to have exerted himself enough. The sapling fell from his hands and rolled over the edge, too. He sat down heavily, upper body heaving as he fought for breath.

'My God!' Gavin was horrified at the cold way the Rafferty men had been pushed off the ledge. 'I-I've never seen anything like this! It – it's barbaric! Just who are you?'

The stranger's face suddenly straightened and he stared long and silently at Gavin before finally whispering hoarsely, 'I-I dunno who I . . . am . . . or what I'm doin' here.'

CHAPTER 3

TAKE CARE

Sean Rafferty was in his mid-fifties and he had a head of black, silver-streaked hair that would have made any lion on the African plains mighty proud.

His face was rugged, yet wasn't as weathered as you might expect for a man his age who had worked outdoors in the West: the lines more clearly defined, not so wrinkled. And the eyes were a piercing brown with clear lenses, like those of a hunting eagle.

Average height but with a barrel chest, his voice was deep and easy-on-the ear with a faint Irish lilt that would never fade. But that voice could take on the cutting edge of an executioner's sword when he was riled.

Right now his clear eyes were narrowed as he stood on the porch of his large riverstone-and-log ranch house set atop a hogback rise commanding a fine view up the twisting length of the Viper River Valley. It was a view that reminded him daily of the emerald green fields of Ireland that he had left so long ago – and that he hoped to see again in the not-too-distant future – providing his plans went as they should. Now he tore his eyes from the valley, standing at the top of the short stone steps, hand-made leather riding boots spread, and looked down at the three battered men waiting there.

'And aren't you a sorry-looking lot,' he said calmly, studying them without any trace of sympathy. 'Clay, you're nominated as spokesman.'

McColl and Lindsey wanted to speak, too, but they had learned long since that that was the wrong way to go about staying in Rafferty's good books. Claiborne shuffled forward so he could reach out an arm and steady himself against the porch upright. His face was bruised and cut, his clothes torn, his boots filthy with both mud and dust and traces of alkali: telling their own story about where he had been.

In thick, halting words, he told his boss about his meeting with Gavin Leach and the mysterious stranger they had watched Leach haul in from the edge of the desert.

'Blind-sided us, chief,' Claiborne finished. 'Hit me with some kind a tree according to Mac.'

'Saplin',' McColl murmured, not looking at Rafferty.

'And . . . ?' Rafferty's bushy white eybrows lifted in a query.

Claiborne sniffed and spat to one side. 'Musta kicked us off the ledge. Lucky it was only a six-foot drop to the next one down.'

Rafferty said nothing, stood staring a moment longer, then turned and went to a high-backed rattan chair. He sat down, prepared a cigar leisurely, leaving the injured and near-exhausted men standing in the hot sun.

'Out at Midget Mountain, you say?' Claiborne nodded dully, wishing he could go stretch out on his bunk – or grab a shotgun and go blast that goddamn stranger to hell. 'Then they *were* on our land but I guess that kid wouldn't know. He's only been with Angie for a few weeks. Still, you did right to challenge him. But this stranger.' Rafferty's eyes narrowed again as he bored his gaze into Claiborne. 'Pretty tough, eh?'

'He blind-sided me!' Claiborne reiterated, straightening and you could tell it wasn't anything he was going to forget in a long while, what that stranger had done to him.

Sean Rafferty waved it away with one clean, long-fingered hand. He puffed on his thick cigar. 'You know for sure the kid brought him in from the desert? He wasn't shamming? I mean definitely an accidental arrival? You'd say that. . . ?'

Claiborne was uneasy. He had had past experience of committing himself and later having it go wrong. Rafferty's wrath was nothing to toy with.

'I can only tell you what I seen, chief,' he answered lamely. 'We seen him earlier in the desert, waited to see what the kid'd do.'

'Hmmm. And he took him back to A-Bar-W?'

'I – dunno. They was gone when we come round – and they'd run off our broncs so we had to walk goddamn miles!'

Rafferty merely stood and started for the door of

the house. 'Saddle my palomino and get yourself cleaned up.'

'Aw, Judas, chief! I need rest and a wash and. . . .'

Claiborne let the words trail off – the rancher had taken absolutely no notice of his protest.

'D'you think he really has lost his memory?'

Angie Bancroft rubbed her hands down her apron-fronted dress and worry lines etched between her eyes as she asked her young brother about the stranger who was now resting on one of the beds in what had once been the children's room at the back of the house.

Gavin sipped his coffee and shrugged. 'He could've, sis. You saw that bump and cut on his head.'

Angie nodded, pushed stray strands of deep brown hair back from her hazel eyes. 'Yes – I'd believe he has some degree of concussion and that could bring on memory loss – temporary or long-term, but – I have to be careful, Gay. Sean Rafferty is a devious man. I wouldn't put it past him to try something like this just to plant his man close to me.'

Leach scoffed. 'Drawing rather a long bow, aren't you, Sis?'

Her eyes glinted. 'Dammit, Gavin! You don't know! You've been away all the time Rafferty's been here, hounding not just me, but the whole valley! He's bought out a lot of settlers and now he wants my land – and I don't want to sell. At any price. He's going to crowd me till I do! And I have to fight him off by any means I can come up with!'

'OK, sis, OK! Calm down. You don't have to sell if you don't want to, so why get worked-up?'

Angie made an effort and forced a smile, reached out to touch his arm. 'I'm sorry. It's very – worrying – and it killed Walt.'

'*Killed* Walt? I thought he had a riding accident?'

She sat down opposite him at the deal table. 'Gav, it's one reason why I didn't keep at you to go back to school. I-I'm worried. All right, *scared*, at times. Walt was worried, too, and very edgy. You know what he was like. He'd stand up to anything that threatened his family, but he admitted to me that Rafferty had him really worried with his persistence and that hard-case crew of his.'

'Well, why does Rafferty want this place so badly? It's nothing special, is it?'

'Something to do with the valley as a whole – I'm not sure. He spoke once about bringing the desert back to life, which, of course, would take a massive amount of water.' Then she added quietly, 'Walt said he thought Rafferty wants to flood the valley, build a damn across from Midget Mountain to Isolation Peak. . . .'

'Good God! That'd be a massive undertaking!'

'Yes. Walt was checking with some of his contacts amongst the engineers back east to see if Rafferty has backing we know nothing about. The day after he sent his telegraph, he had his – accident. . . .'

'But that's what it was, Sis, wasn't it? An accident?' Gavin looked very worried now, felt his belly knot.

'Sheriff Nichols was supposed to be investigating, but – well, they call him 'Windy' Nichols and he is mostly talk – and also a good friend of Sean Rafferty's.'

Gavin finished his coffee, stood and came round to stand beside his sister, slipping an arm across her shoulders. 'Sis, you've had a helluva lot of worry this last year or so, what with losing the children and then Walt. You've done what you always do: bottle up your troubles, try to solve them yourself.'

'It's my way, Gavin. Always has been. I can't help it.'

'Yes! And it's a wonder you haven't got a headful of grey hair! But you don't have to do that this time. Walt's gone, but I'm here. Oh, sure, I'm a green-horn, but I remember something of ranch work when I was a kid before you sent me away to school – I can help, I want to and I *will*. If I have to learn how to handle a gun, I'll do that, too.'

She stood, turned to him and put her arms around him, kissing his cheek, standing on tiptoe to do it. 'Thank you, Gav. I-I guess I need *someone*.'

'And it's me, I'm—' He broke off, looking past her out of the window. He stepped back and she frowned, turning quickly. 'Well, we can soon find out just what Rafferty's plans are. Here he comes down the trail now.'

Angie pulled aside the curtain a little and said, with maybe a slight tremor in her voice, 'Yes – and he's got Claiborne with him!'

Rafferty doffed his fine-looking hat, a Western hat hand-made back East, as he sat his big palomino with easy grace and nodded courteously to Angie where she waited on her porch, Gavin beside her.

'Fine day, Mrs Bancroft.'

'It was shaping-up that way till I saw you and your tame coyote riding in.'

Claiborne scowled, his bruised face and swollen neck hurting with the effort. Angie looked vaguely amused.

'Why, I think you've somehow improved your looks, Claiborne. Whatever did you do to your face?'

The big man bared his teeth, thick lips peeling back, but Rafferty chuckled and spoke, cutting off Clay's reply. 'He does look rather different. Thanks to your new hand, I believe.'

That startled Angie and she blinked. It was Gavin who replied, 'We don't have any new hands, Rafferty.'

'Oh? I heard you went to meet someone out in the basin and brought him back here.'

'He was hurt! Claiborne and his friends saw him *yesterday* in trouble and didn't lift a finger to help him.'

Rafferty shook his head, lips pursed. 'Well, that's not like Clay – or this legendary "Code Of The West" you hear so much about—'

'I didn't think you'd even heard of it, 'Angie cut in suddenly and Rafferty sobered, looking briefly annoyed.

He made the smile come back. 'I won't take up much of your time, Mrs Bancroft, I just wanted you to understand that I don't intend to make any trouble about your brother's trespass on—'

'Trespass?'

'On my land near Midget Mountain. Clay was

trying to explain the boundaries to him when your man – er – this *stranger* he had befriended, attacked my men with a club.' He shook his head slowly. 'I don't want any kind of trouble – you've certainly had your share, lately. I don't intend to add to it.'

'You've wasted your time coming here, Mr Rafferty,' Angie told him coolly. 'You know as well as I do what really happened at Midget Mountain, so, I won't keep you any longer.'

She turned abruptly to the house door but Rafferty said sharply, 'Just one moment!' His voice was crisp, peremptory, but when she turned slowly, he brought back the smile. 'One more time, Mrs Bancroft, will you consider my offer for your ranch? Please? Surely you must admit it's more than generous.'

Angie stared down at him and his smile slowly faded. 'It is, as you say, Mr Rafferty, *more* than generous, which makes me wonder just why you want my land so badly.'

The smile returned but there was a stiffness around the edges now. 'Mrs Bancroft, I'm not sure that I can explain but – well, my grandfather founded a coach-making business in Dublin, built it up and sold out to competition, then migrated to America. But my father, the eldest son, stayed behind with my stepmother. The Estate was to be sold but somehow that bitch of a stepmother cheated us out of our heritage.' He paused to settle his breathing. 'While she destroyed our estate with her excesses, in America, my grandfather and uncles built a business empire in Boston and New York, invested in a railroad in which they eventually owned the majority of shares. A true land of opportunity, eh?'

Gavin whistled softly, but Rafferty waited in vain for the woman to express any interest. 'My cousins are partners in that railroad but because of – well, an unjust family decision, I, and my father were not admitted. So, after his death, I set out on my own to prove that I, too, had inherited the Rafferty business acumen, drive and ambition.'

'Buying my ranch will help you achieve this?' Angie asked sceptically and Rafferty flushed slightly at her tone.

'You may be surprised, but yes! It will. You see, it is my intention to show my family I, too, can leave something enduring and worthwhile for this great country.' His eyes sparkled and he lowered his voice. 'I am now in my fifties and I have – accrued – a considerable amount of money so profit is not the major interest here. I intend to revive the Carnaby Desert! Turn it into lush pastures for herds of fine beef cattle, forests of usable timber, land families will be proud to settle and perhaps, even reminiscent of my homeland, that green Ireland of my child-hood—'

'A fantasy,' cut in Gavin.

Rafferty, eyes narrowed, looked at him coldly, unsmiling.

'So most people think, young man, but it can be done. *I* can do it! And I will do it! I have investors back East, just waiting in the wings for me to give the go-ahead.' He turned back to Angie. 'Only you and the Pritchards are holding out, but I think Tate

Pritchard is finally starting to see good sense – so you can see why I need your land, now, Mrs Bancroft – Angie, if I may call you that?'

' "Mrs Bancroft" will do. I think I do see why you want my land – you're going to flood the valley, aren't you? Just as Walt predicted.'

Rafferty didn't like her being that much of a jump ahead of him but he finally raised a finger and wagged it at her, smiling again.

'I knew you were a smart woman, Mrs Bancroft! Yes, it will be necessary to flood the Viper River Valley in its entirety, turn it into a huge man-made lake and dam.'

'Which is why you built your place so high up, no doubt?'

'Yes, I admit to that. This has been a long-term project for me – and I should mention that there is a good deal of government backing available, providing we meet certain criteria and deadlines.' He suddenly spread his arms. 'Well, I have been candid. If you still refuse to consider my offer, will you do me the courtesy of being candid with me as to your reasons for refusal?'

'Certainly – there are only two, Mr Rafferty. First, my husband sweated long and hard to build this ranch for me and his family. We were his life—'

'And you feel an obligation to carry on and see that his – vision – is realized.' Rafferty nodded several times. 'Yes, I can understand that. Very commendable indeed. And the second reason?'

Angie's face was very tight and a little pale as she said, 'My husband and children are buried here on this land.'

It took Rafferty a little time to understand and then his face registered shock and he frowned and he tried twice before he could speak.

'You – are you saying. . . ? Good God, woman! Is that why you've held us up for months, put us well behind schedule, because of a few *graves*?'

'My husband and children's graves! Not just any graves, damn you!' Angie snapped, and he waved irritably, failing in his rising anger, to see the cold, stubborn look turning her features to stone.

'My dear woman, I am quite willing to see that your family is disinterred with all propriety and moved to a safer, more suitable place, well above water level. If this is your major objection – well, I only wish you had mentioned it earlier! It could've been overcome in a few minutes!'

'*No!*' Angie's single word was said with such force and hostility that Rafferty actually reared back in his saddle, startled at her vehemence. She leaned over the porch rail. 'My family are resting where they should be and their peace will not be disturbed under any circumstances!'

'Good grief, woman, I've assured you it will be done in the best of tastes. I'll arrange for a preacher of your choice, for re-interrment. I'll even supply suitable new caskets—'

'*Get off my land!*'

Gavin stepped forward and took his sister's arm as she leaned far over the rail to hurl the words in Rafferty's face. This time he didn't rear back, but his frown deepened and Claiborne said quietly, 'I can handle this, chief, just say the word.'

Rafferty lifted a cautionary hand without looking at his foreman. 'Mrs Bancroft, if you would calm down a moment or two, we can sit down and discuss this reasonably—'

'My sister told you to get off our land, Rafferty!' Gavin said, cursing as that nervous tremor rattled his voice. He wished he was wearing a gun or had a rifle handy. His heart was hammering and Claiborne curled a lip.

'You'd best stay outa this, kid.' He dropped a hand to his gun butt, then stiffened and Angie heard a cold, rasping voice behind her say, 'Best do what the lady wants, mister!'

The words were followed by a cold metallic snapping sound that meant only one thing – a gun hammer had been cocked

She spun, as did Gavin, and they stared at the battered stranger swaying in the doorway, one shoulder pressed against the frame, holding a double-barrelled shotgun in his scarred hands, the bruised wrists showing plainly.

He was watching Claiborne and Rafferty, jerked the gun barrels a couple of inches. 'Trail's over yonder – I'll give you a slow count of three to get moving.'

Rafferty's face was cold and vicious. 'So you're the desert stranger I've been hearing about.'

'He's got the luck of the devil, chief! The desert should've finished him and if he hadn't blind-sided me I . . .'

Claiborne's words trailed off and the others, too, saw the way the man had tensed at Claiborne's words.

41

'You have a name, friend?' queried Rafferty tautly.

The man looked at him bleakly. 'Your sidekick said I'm "lucky" – that's good enough. Call me "Lucky". Now, one – two – thr—'

By then Rafferty and Claiborne were wheeling their horses and riding across the yard towards the hills and the trail back to Rafferty's ranch.

The man slumped, the gun pointing floorwards, and Gavin stepped forward to support him. 'That gun's not even loaded, you know that?'

The man called 'Lucky' nodded wearily.

'Heard voices – sounded unfriendly. Found the gun in a cupboard. Couldn't find the shells. . . .'

His legs suddenly gave way and Gavin Leach grunted as he took his weight.

'Put him back on Joel's bed, Gavin. I'll get some warm water and clean him up properly – and we'll see what he has to say for himself.'

Angie held the door while Gavin struggled through with the big, inert stranger.

What kind of man was this? she wondered. A man who would knowingly face armed strangers with an empty shot-gun.

CHAPTER 4

'GET TOUGH!'

Link Cady didn't like this 'Lucky' son of a bitch. He decided almost as soon as he set eyes on the battered stranger as he sat around on the porch smoking, head bandaged, raking those scary eyes around the yard. He had walked around for a while, limping, and Link figured it wouldn't be long before he was in the saddle, poking his nose into every corner of the A-Bar-W.

Link had his reasons for not wanting that. He could manage the greenhorn kid, no problem, but this new one looked mighty tough. Well, Cady was a tough man in his own right, too, had been kicked about since he could walk, when he first went to the orphanage. It was a case of take it and cower and make life more miserable than it already was, or find some way of fighting back.

By the time he was eight years old, Link knew how he could get back at all the 'guardians' who had beat on him and abused him, men and women. They gave him a job in the kitchen filling the coffee and tea for a luncheon spread the orphanage was providing for visiting do-gooders. Only two days before he had discovered where the iron-jawed matron kept the Epsom Salts that she dosed the kids with when they fussed . . . so he added a liberal – *very* liberal – quantity of the salts to the urns. In the general chaos that ensued, Link ran away, jumped a train west, and had made his own way ever since.

Link walked across to where Gavin Leach was saddling a horse at the corrals.

'Him on the porch – he stayin' on? Looks like he thinks he's the new boss.'

Gavin looked sharply at Cady. 'Don't be stupid. Sis is just letting him rest up until he's feeling better. He's taken a hell of a beating in that desert, crossed it north to south.'

Link snorted. 'He *says*!'

'Why would he lie? And Sis says it's the only way he could've gotten to the section of the basin I found him in.'

'Yeah? Well, what the hell was he doin' in Carnaby Desert in the first place? You think to ask him that?'

'They tell me that you don't pry into a man's business out here, Link. He'll tell us in his own good time or he won't. He hasn't regained his memory yet.'

Again Link snorted. 'You believe that? Listen, I've had my run-ins with tough sheriffs over the years. I've had the cuffs snapped on me just as tight as they'd go – and they left bruises and raw skin on my wrists, just like them on this *hombre*'s wrists. You ask me, he's on the dodge.'

Gavin thinned his lips and turned back to tightening the cinchstrap.

That part had been worrying him, too. . . .

Claiborne's face was still bruised but some of the swelling had gone down and his neck wasn't quite so stiff. But enough discomfort remained to keep his hatred for 'Lucky' burning at red heat.

He sniffed and spat before mounting the steps to the big ranch house, went inside and down the passage to where Rafferty awaited him in what he called his den.

The walls were decorated with the heads of reindeer, mountain lion and one bear, fierce in expression with the enlarged teeth the taxidermist had given it. Fancy weapons were set in racks: Purdey hand-made shotguns with filigree gold and silver wire decorations; Harrison & Richardson hunting rifles with engraved bolts and actions; ornate revolvers in glass-fronted cases. Interspersed between the weapons were paintings of Ireland, one of an ancient castle with partially crumbled walls in a large ornate gilt frame. Claiborne figured that if ever he quit here, he would take along some of those fancy guns. . . .

'Ah, Clay,' Rafferty greeted his ramrod, looking up from a pile of mail that had been brought to him from town. 'What have you found out about that hardcase at the Bancroft place?'

'Nothin' yet, chief. I've seen Windy Nichols. He's sendin' wires all over the place, but says he ain't had any word of prisoners on the run in this neck of the woods.'

The rancher made an exasperated sound. 'Dammit! The man came in across the desert! That's not "this neck of the woods"! Tell Nichols to start looking further afield. I saw those marks on his wrists, they were still raw. That ranny's escaped custody from somewhere not long ago – and I want to know *where* and when.'

Claiborne nodded. 'OK, but I don't see the worry, chief. He's tough, but I figure he just bought into that deal because Angie'd been takin' care of him – I don't think she sent for him, if that's what's botherin' you.'

It was quiet in the room for what seemed like a long time to Claiborne.

'I – don't know, 'Rafferty admitted slowly. 'But I can't take the chance of someone coming in here to start snooping around.' He tapped the letter he had been reading when the ramrod had entered. 'From the group in Chicago – they're tightening the deadline. They want returns on their investment, *pronto*. We know there have been complaints about the way we – acquired some of the land around here – They may not be provable but one of the law agencies could be suspicious enough to send in someone to check things out.'

Claiborne arched his eyebrows. 'That drifter? With them 'cuff marks on him. . . ?'

'A good enough cover, don't you think? Make us believe he's on the run from the law.'

The ramrod thought Rafferty was paranoid, although that wasn't a word in his vocabulary, but he figured that the big Irish son of a bitch was being

46

hassled by his 'friends' back East and jumping at every shadow that didn't seem to fit in place around here.

He said nothing.

'I want to know what he's doing on the Bancroft place, Clay. If he saddles-up and rides out within the next few days, have someone follow him, though I must admit I'll feel quite a relief if that's what he does. It'll mean he's just been recuperating there as it appears and is moving on. But if he starts snooping around – well, I'll certainly want to know that, too!'

'Whatever you say, chief.' Claiborne paused at the door. 'If Angie won't sell because she don't want the family graves flooded – well, d'you have to pussyfoot around with her? Why not move in rough, get tough, run her off, and that greenhorn kid brother with her.'

Rafferty smiled thinly. 'I'm tempted, Clay, oh, believe me, *I am sorely tempted* to do just that, but it will be prudent to satisfy ourselves about this stranger first.'

As Claiborne nodded and went out, he murmured, 'Prudent, my ass. I'd as soon put a bullet in him right now and settle it for sure.'

Lucky was at the wash bench near the kitchen door when he saw Gavin walking towards the corrals, carrying a rifle. Angie was hanging out washing nearby and, as he patted his sore face dry – it was still sun-raw and tender – he said, 'First time I've seen the kid with a gun. Is he any good with it?'

Angie took a wooden clothes peg from between

47

her teeth and pushed it over the folds of a dress on the strung rope of the line. She looked at the man for a moment before shaking her head.

'I think he's not a bad shot but he doesn't like guns much.'

'Then why's he toting one?' The stranger gestured to where Gavin was now sliding the rifle into a scabbard and attaching it by rawhide thongs to the saddle.

'He saw some of Rafferty's riders on our land yesterday. They rode away when he tried to approach them and ask what they were doing.'

Lucky nodded, eyes narrowing as he watched the kid. He started forward around the side of the house, saying quietly, 'He's tying it on all wrong . . .' He raised his voice. 'Hey, kid! Wait up.'

Gavin turned as he saw Lucky coming towards him, still limping slightly. 'You're walking better.'

'Getting there. Gavin, you've tied that scabbard wrong. The rifle's upside down in it and it's tilted too low. Your breech'll be full of grit and dust in no time – and water if it rains.'

As he spoke he shouldered Gavin aside, untied the rawhide thongs, arranged the scabbard at a slight downward angle, butt towards the rear.

Gavin frowned, hesitated, then said quietly, 'I thought the butt should be facing forward?'

'That's OK – in dry country. But you come from a place that gets a lot of rain like me, you have it this way, butt angled up and to the rear. You might have to lean a mite to free the gun, but you can drape your slicker folds over it and keep it dry, too. Worth that

48

extra effort to twist and lean. A gun that works is what you want, not one jammed with grit or rusting from too much water.'

Gavin nodded his thanks. Gathering the reins, one boot in stirrup, he asked casually, 'You speak from experience, I take it?'

Lucky hesitated, rubbed at his head bandage. 'Well – it seems to be just something I know. Where you headed, kid?'

Gavin swung into the saddle. 'Just riding. Familiarizing myself with the place – I don't want to make the mistake of crossing Rafferty's line again.' He smiled. 'You might not be around to rescue me.'

The stranger shrugged that off. 'Hardly recollect doing anything. Just reacted, I guess. How about I come with you?'

'Well, d'you feel up to it?'

'You saddle me a horse and I'll see if I can borrow a hat and some more of Walt's clothes – he seems to've been about my size. . . .' As he started back to the house, Gavin dismounted, looped his reins over the corral rail and ran his eyes over the remuda, wondering what kind of horse to pick for Lucky Whoever-he-was.

He chose a claybank and had it saddled and waiting when Lucky came back, wearing a checked shirt and whipcord trousers, both of which had belonged to Walt Bancroft, but his boots were his own.

Gavin knew, too, that it was Walt's old Colt, complete with bullet belt and holster, that the man carried in his left hand. He paused and buckled it on and Gavin frowned. Lucky did it with such ease and even a certain amount of grace, so that when the holster settled and he tied down the base to his leg, the gun rig looked right at home. And the way Lucky set the weapon in the holster told Gavin that here was a man used to guns and quite at home with them.

'Let's go,' he said and mounted the claybank. 'We find a lonely draw, we'll take a little time out and I'll show you how to shoot – OK?'

Gavin said nothing as he mounted his own horse. But his heart was beating faster. He'd never felt easy about guns somehow. . . .

And Angie stared over the sheet she was hanging on the clothes line, noticing that gun on the stranger's hip, looking a little apprehensive.

From behind the barn, Link Cady watched, too, pursing his lips thoughtfully, as the two men rode out.

Gavin Leach knew of a couple of isolated draws that he had found on his rides around A-Bar-W but he didn't go near them during the morning, showing Lucky where he had figured out the boundaries to be.

'Pretty big place,' the man allowed. 'Lush valley – be a pity to see it disappear under water.'

'Well, yes. But I guess you can see where govern- ment would be interested in such a scheme to bring the desert back to life.'

'What? Flood this fertile valley, to bring life to a desert not much bigger?' Lucky shook his head. 'Don't make much sense to me – Think of how much it'd cost.'

Gavin nodded. 'Yes, I have. At college we touched

on a little engineering, along with several other subjects, just giving us a taste to see who might be interested in what, you know? I reckon it'd take hundreds of thousands to pull off. . . . But, of course, the dam wouldn't be used just for the desert, there's all that country to the west and south that could benefit if pipelines were built.'

'You're talking about things on a mighty big scale, kid. You ask me, it's Rafferty's ego that's bigger'n anything else.'

Leach snapped his head around. 'What? You mean – you think he's doing it for *his own satisfaction*?'

Lucky shrugged. 'His family have left their mark, way back, if you can believe him. He seems to be on the outer with his family. Could be he sees this as a chance to show 'em all that he can leave his mark on this country, too – and no doubt make a good profit as well.'

Gavin blew out his cheeks. 'Seems a bit far-fetched if you ask me,' he allowed but Lucky didn't seem to hear.

'That looks like the entrance to a draw yonder,' he said. 'Let's go see . . .'

It was a draw and Lucky insisted that they set things up so he could give Gavin some lessons in firearms' handling.

'Look, I don't like guns. . . .'

'Then why bring that rifle?'

'Well, I am a bit uneasy riding alone out here.'

'If you don't know how to use a gun, kid, leave it at home – or take time to learn. What'll it be?'

Gavin hesitated, licked his lips and finally nodded.

'I guess I want to be able to protect Angie, and if it means learning how to shoot then so be it. I suppose you know what you're doing, Lucky.'

Gavin said this a little strangely and Lucky merely grunted and began pacing out a range.

He set up stones and chips of wood, a broken whiskey bottle Gavin found by a rock, and even some of the shards of shattered glass.

'Kind of small, aren't they?'

'They'll catch the light and reflect it – make a good target, practice for shooting against the sun, too, but it's not something I'd recommend. OK. First piece of wood's on that hummock, twenty feet away. Shoot at it with the rifle.'

He had to show the kid how to hold the Winchester properly, get the metal curve of the butt snugly into his shoulder so as to save bruising, to grip firmly.

'Hold that fore-grip with your left hand cupped, fingers wrapped around the wood, then pull back firmly – not too hard or your fingers'll go numb and you lose the feel of the gun – OK. Sight so that the tip of the foreblade settles dead-centre in the V of the rear sight, but level with the top of the arms . . . *level* with the top of the V! You shoot like that, and you'll only dig a hole at the base of the hummock. Not too high, damnit! You're not trying to bring down that hawk. OK. That's reasonable – now squeeze the trigger – don't jerk – Jesus, I said *don't jerk!*'

The rifle crashed and the sound batted at their ears and the horses started and snorted – and nothing happened to the piece of wood. No dirt even sprayed from the hummock.

But way down the line, the bullet ricocheted from a lichen-scabbed boulder and chewed a handful of dirt from the high edge of the draw.

'What happened?' Gavin asked, bewildered. 'I sighted just as you said. . . .'

'But you *jerked* the trigger like you were trying to pull it out of the action! *Squeeze*! You ever give a girl a little squeeze round the waist, sort of testing the lie of the land for something a bit more intimate later? No? Well, kid, you got a *lot* to learn – and, it seems, not just about guns!'

Gavin flushed. 'All right, all right! Let's stick to the subject . . . I shot wrong. Well, show me how to do it right! Now we've started I might as well do the best I can.'

Lucky smiled thinly. 'Good attitude, kid.'

Time ran away.

It was afternoon and the draw stank of powder-smoke, was filled with tendrils of grey fog. The small hummocks closest to the men were ragged lumps of dirt, diminished in size from all the bullets chewing away at them. The whiskey bottle was in pieces. Smaller sections of glass were no more than splinters. Slabs of bark were riddled and twigs were splintered enough to be used as tooth picks.

Gavin complained his trigger finger had a blister on it and his hands were cramped and his shoulder was bruised.

'That's when you lost your concentration,' Lucky told him without sympathy. 'You gotta *think* when you're shooting. Right now you'll have to do it

53

consciously. With a little practice, all I've taught you will come naturally.'

'When? By the time my hair turns grey?'

Lucky grinned, punched Gavin lightly on the sore shoulder and the kid winced and swore, rubbing hard.

'You're not a bad shot. Need lots of practice, but doing OK.'

Leach blinked, surprised. 'Then why've you been cussing me so much? Telling me what a lousy shot I am?'

'Make sure you stayed awake. You looked kinda bleary-eyed there for a while.'

'Maybe you were boring me!'

Lucky conceded that with a grin and a shrug. 'Well, kid, like I said, you did OK – for the first lesson. We'll do a little each day till you can hit what you aim at five times outa six – you want to try a six-gun, by the way?'

Gavin shook his head vigorously. 'Not today, thank you!' Then something seemed to occur to him. 'You haven't showed me what you can do with a gun.'

Lucky was sober now. 'Throwing down a chal-lenge, eh? Well, let's see . . .' He reached out and took the rifle from Gavin, glanced up, then threw the Winchester to his shoulder and fired.

Gavin squinted, shading his eyes, saw an eruption of feathers and the mangled body of a hunting hawk in its final swoop on its target hurtling to the ground.

'My God! That bird must've been moving at forty miles an hour!'

'All in how you lead a moving target, kid.'

He threw up the rifle again and lever and trigger worked in smooth blurs as shot after shot rent the heat of afternoon. The short, splintered neck of the bottle disintegrated, sticks no larger than half the length of a man's little finger leapt wildly into the air, individual stones no bigger than a thumbnail shattered and buzzed.

Gavin was impressed and his eyes were slightly wide as he turned to Lucky who was already reloading the rifle's magazine.

'Never be caught with an empty gun, kid. If you can, leave one shot always and reload quick as possible.'

'All right. How about the Colt? Are you any good?'

'Average.'

Lucky pointed to a small bush with his left hand, and then the Colt was banging and slamming in his right fist and the bush was stripped of its thin branches and leaves one by one. He stopped shooting at five and dropped the loading gate for Gavin to see that he had left one cartridge in the cylinder, ready to come up under the hammer.

'Precaution.'

'You seem to know all this stuff like an expert – I don't suppose I should ask but were you ever a lawman?'

Lucky laughed. 'Me? Not me, kid.'

Gavin Gavin sobered. 'Then – you learnt all this on the *other* side of the law?'

'Now why would you ask a man such a thing?' Lucky wanted to know, thumbing home new shells into the Colt. 'Don't you know that could get your head shot off?'

'I – er – I knew it was risky but I wanted to know – still do. You're an intriguing man, Lucky.'

'I've been called lots of things, but never that, far as I can remember.' He glanced up at the sky and the heeled-over sun. 'Guess we better be heading back. . . .'

As they mounted and turned towards the mouth of the draw, Gavin put his mount alongside the clay-bank and, when Lucky looked at him, said, 'You haven't lost your memory at all, have you?'

Lucky's face didn't change but he didn't answer.

'You've made a couple of mistakes – said you came from a place that had a lot of rain – are a bit too adamant that you were never a lawman; something of "methinks he protesteth too much", if the Bard will forgive me – and at supper last night when Sis asked if you wanted chilli sauce on your steak you said, "I never use it – Did once in Mexico at a *hidalgo's* fiesta, made me sick on the spot. Embarrassing – 'course, I'd had more than my share of tequila, too. I've passed on chilli ever since." Sis didn't appear to notice, but it seemed to me you were recalling details you wouldn't know if you really had lost your memory. . . .'

They had ridden as far as the river before Lucky answered, looking levelly at Gavin Leach.

'Seems like I slipped up, doesn't it, kid? You're a lot damn sharper than I figured.'

CHAPTER 5

MAN OF MYSTERY

Link Cady was riding the river when he saw something in midstream that caught his attention. He couldn't quite make it out, put his mount into the murky water.

Turned out to be a battered old burlap sack with a dead kitten in it. He tossed it away, started to turn his mount, when a voice cracked from the far bank – on the Rafferty side.

'You're trespassin', Cady! No! Hold it right there or I'll shoot. I'm within my rights! You're past the mid-line of the river!'

It was McColl, with Lindsey by his side. Both held rifles on Link and he swallowed, raised his hands and at their instructions, kneed his mount across.

'Listen, fellers, I just seen what I thought was an old hat caught on the edge of the sandbank and . . .'

McColl hit him across the side of the head with his rifle barrel. He swayed in the saddle and Lindsey grabbed the reins and urged Link's mount up onto the bank.

While he was dazed they rode him back through the brush and into a campsite where Claiborne was sitting on a log, smoking, and nursing a tin mug of coffee. The ramrod glanced up and showed interest when he recognized the dazed Link Cady. McColl halted the horses and pushed Cady out of the saddle. He grunted when he hit the ground, rolled over to hands and knees, started to his feet.

But Lindsey kicked him between the shoulders and he staggered forward, fell again to hands and knees only a few feet from Claiborne.

'Trespassin', Clay. Was crossin' the river when we caught him.'

'Now why would you want to do that, Link?'

'I wasn't! An old sack that looked like a hat was caught up, an—' He gasped and clawed at his eyes as Claiborne tossed the remains of his hot coffee at his face.

Claiborne stood, hitched at his trouser belt and brushed a hand across his nostrils, sniffing. 'You better quit lyin', Link, 'cause I'm gonna ask you some questions 'bout the new ranny on A Bar W.'

'Hell, I dunno nothin' about him! Nobody does. Says he's lost his memory.'

'You believe that, Link?'

'I dunno – he was pretty much beat when Gav brought him in. . . .'

'What's he done since?'

Link felt this was progress, co-operating with Claiborne, but he kept his eye on the big, brutal man's fists. 'Nothin' much – too tuckered, I guess.'

'We seen him ridin' with Gav yest'y,' said McColl. He flicked his gaze to Claiborne. 'Heard some shootin' way off, too, Clay.'

The ramrod's eyes narrowed. 'Did you now. How about that, Link? Know anythin' about it?'

Cady licked his lips, nodded. 'Matter of fact, I do. I kinda followed Gav and this Lucky as he calls hisself. They just rode for a spell, then went into a draw and – you ready for this? – Lucky give the kid a whole bunch of shootin' lessons: how to handle a rifle and a six-gun. They was there for hours.'

The three Rafferty men exchanged glances and Claiborne asked, 'He do any shootin' hisself? This Lucky, I mean.'

Link snorted, smiling crookedly. 'I should smile he did! Man, he's a dead shot with a rifle – and as for a six-gun. Well, I never even seen him draw and he stripped a small bush of its leaves and branches, Colt blastin' like a Gatlin' gun!'

Again the Rafferty men exchanged glances. McColl and Lindsey looked a mite worried, but Claiborne kept his face blank.

'Would you tag him as a gunfighter?'

Link stiffened: he hadn't expected that question and he looked thoughtful before answering. 'Ye-ah – yeah! I would! That's exactly what I'd call him, the way he used them weapons – a goddamn gunfighter!'

Claiborne poured more coffee from the black-ened, bubbling pot and Link stiffened, but the man took a couple of sips, looking at Cady steadily.

'So Angie's hired herself a fast gun. . . .'

Link looked startled. 'Well – I dunno as she's *hired* him.'

'He's there, ain't he? Workin' for her, teachin' the kid how to shoot.'

'He's still recoverin' from crossin' the Carnaby.'

'But Gavin brought him in, eh? How you know the kid wasn't *s'posed* to meet him out there? Feller lost his hoss, mebbe, had to make the rest of the way afoot and was lucky enough to be picked up by the kid.' He snorted again, spat. 'That's where the "Lucky" comes in, eh? He coulda died out there.'

'Almost did, accordin' to Angie.'

Claiborne drank a gulp of coffee. 'Ye-ah – Angie – well, if she's hirin' gunfighters, she sure ain't ready to sell and the chief wants her place pronto.' He stood suddenly, tossed his coffe into the fire, much to Link's relief. 'Link, old son, I'm the one s'posed to make Angie see reason and if I don't Mr Rafferty'll gut and flay me alive – I got no hankerin' for that, so tell you what I'm gonna do.'

On the last word, he swung a boot viciously into Link's face. The man lifted completely off his hands and knees and rolled almost into the fire. Claiborne stepped up, nudged him into the edge of the flames and coals with a boot, holding him there. Link screamed, shirt smouldering.

McColl and Lindsey looked uncomfortable as they smelled burning flesh. Then Claiborne eased up the pressure and Link, sobbing, pushed himself back.

'Mac, Lin – hold this son of a bitch upright.'

By the time they had obeyed, Claiborne had pulled on a pair of sweat-hardened leather work-

gloves and he faced the sagging Cady, no longer the
tough young ranny he liked to think he was.

'You don't work for Angie no more, Link,'
Claiborne told the frightened man. 'You don't work
for no one around here. When I'm finished with you
here, you just ride on outa the valley and don't come
back – you savvy?'

Link just stared out of pain-filled eyes, nodded
slowly.

Then Claiborne grinned crookedly and said, 'If
you can ride, that is . . .' And the first blow took Link
in the midriff and contorted his features as he
gagged and retched.

Claiborne moved his boots wide, settled his shoulders and began swinging blow after blow into the
cowboy's body, working up to his face, stepping
around him to slam punches into his kidneys and
spine. McColl and Lindsey cursed the sagging
cowboy, snarling at him to 'Stand up!' but Link's
rubbery legs wouldn't hold him.

After a while, breathing hard, sniffing and hawk-
ing, Claiborne wiped a sleeve across his nostrils and
gasped, 'Let him drop.'

McColl and Lindsey released Link and he fell on
his face, shuddering, blood on the ground under
him, his clothes torn and red-soaked, his breathing
sounding wet and slobbering.

Then Claiborne started in with his boots.

At supper the previous night, in the kitchen of
Angie's house, with old Horseshoe dragging his
wooden leg as he served what he called his 'sono-

61

fabitch stew', one of his prized, ex-traildrive recipes, the man called 'Lucky' sipped some water from the glass beside him and saw Angie and Gavin staring at him expectantly.

'OK, my name's Lucky Montana. Well, "Lucky" was tagged onto me by some tinhorn a while back and it's kind of stuck. Montana's a family name. Spanish, somewheres way back.'

'And why did you say you'd lost your memory, Mr Montana?' Angie asked, somewhat frostily.

'Habit – I like to know who I'm with and the surroundings before I admit to anything. Even my name.'

'I guess that's fair enough, Sis.'

Angie didn't look at her brother, kept her gaze on Lucky's still bruised face. 'It sounds to me the way a man who has something to hide might act.'

Lucky drank some more water, toyed with the glass, gaze lowered, not answering.

'I know I'm not supposed to pry, Mr Montana, but you're staying in my house and I believe I have a right to know something at least of your background – your true background.'

He nodded, sighed. 'I guess – OK. Could be I'm on the dodge.'

'*Could* be?'

He stared at her now, soberly, eyes flat and unreadable. He turned the almost empty glass between his fingers. Gavin waited, leaning forward a little in his tension. Angie met and held Lucky's gaze and tried to hide the discomfort she felt.

She sensed that here was a mighty dangerous man.

'Come from up north – a long ways north. I've been in some trouble. Found it hard to settle after the war and got in with a bad bunch. . . .'

'Of course!' she said sardonically. 'It wasn't your fault, you were just led astray!'

His cold eyes never wavered. 'No, I was the leader of the bad bunch,' he said flatly, and she showed her surprise as Gavin whistled softly. 'Never mind that – it was a long time ago and I've tamed down some since. Got married.'

'Ah! Of course! The good woman! You seem to have been reading the same books I have, Mr Montana. Full of clichés!'

His face was bleak now and she knew she had ragged him just a little too much.

'She *was* a good woman. But she died. And I went out and killed the man who caused her death. Trouble was, he had a lot of important friends and they hired a gunfighter named Dawson so I had to go on the run. He nearly caught me at Rapid City, Dakota, and then some damn lawman picked me up for stealing the horse I got away on in a dump called Murphy's Creek. . . .'

'You do have rather bad luck, don't you?' She didn't sound so sarcastic now, regarded him more thoughtfully.

He nodded. 'That's why I say the nickname never did fit. Anyway, this lawman decided to take me back to Casper, Wyoming, where the Cattlemen's Association would pay him a bounty for the return of one of their horses – and use me as an example to anyone else with ideas of stealing one of their broncs

– makin' sure they'd forget all about 'em, pronto.'

He put a hand round his neck, grimaced hideously.

'They – they were going to hang you?' Gavin asked, frowning, and when Lucky nodded, said, 'Without a trial?'

'Never got that far. Some wild bunch hit the train we were on and he was convinced they were trying to rescue me. We left the train and made a run through the timber, but came out on a cliff top over a river – seventy feet straight down.' He paused and they could see his thoughts turn inwards as he relived that heart-stopping moment. 'Damn fool panicked, grabbed my arm and jumped, dragging me with him.'

'*Seventy feet!*' exclaimed Gavin Leach.

'Felt like seven hundred before we hit the river,' admitted Montana slowly, remembering. . . .

Wind rushed past hard enough to whip the hat from his head, almost turning his eyeballs inside out.

He would never forget that shocking feeling of his stomach travelling upwards from its normal position into the back of his throat. They began to twist in mid-air and through the blur of wind-induced tears he saw the countryside turn sideways, then upside down, then spin around. He opened his mouth to yell and the wind smashed past his teeth, ballooned his cheeks, roared in his throat and his lungs felt as if they would burst outwards through his ribs.

The sheriff was yelling – and then they hit.

No one could ever tell Lucky Montana that water was soft to land on.

They were lucky inasmuch as they hit a deep part of the river but it felt to Montana as if he had landed on compacted dirt. What breath he had left was smashed from him, the world disappeared in a rocket-trail of stars and bursting lights and his head was filled with a bubbling roar that threatened to explode his brain.

Something hard hit him alongside the head and more red starbursts formed a curtain behind his eyes. It might have been a rock, floating debris, even one of the sheriff's boots, for he could feel the toppling body of his captor tangling with his own flailing limbs.

It got mighty wild after that. Wrenching sensations so that he thought his body was coming apart. He wished his hands were free of the goddamn hand-cuffs and was grateful at least that they were in front of him and not behind his back. He tried his best to use his arms and boots to fend off obstructions. The other man's body didn't seem to want to leave him: it rolled and twisted into his path several times.

Now and again the current thrust him up enough to gasp a lungful of air – he didn't know how the lawman fared in this respect. Underwater the light was murky green, sometimes much darker. He bounced off the river bottom at least a dozen times, feeling the rough gravel shred his clothes – and his skin. 'Up' and 'down' were directions he no longer knew. It was all a swirl and tumbling and twisting and bouncing until finally he began retching sand and water and found he had washed-up on a sandbank. Water was only inches deep over the bar and he had the feeling he had been out to it for a time and was just coming round. His vision was strange, blurred, distorting things, but he recognized the sheriff's body lying a few feet away, legs trailing in the water.

Head throbbing, bleeding from a temple wound, Montana, still gagging, crawled across awkwardly with his manacled hands, the iron cuffs having torn and bruised his wrists badly enough for them to bleed. He rolled the sheriff onto his back – and vomited when he saw the raw, shredded pulp that was all that was left of the man's face. The lawman must have bounced off a lot more rocks than he had. . . .

Afterwards, he searched the body's torn and sodden clothing and found the key to the handcuffs snagged in a corner of a jacket pocket. His fingers were mighty stiff and sore and bleeding but he managed to manipulate the key into the lock of the left cuff and then the right one was easy.

He started to fling the cuffs away, paused, made himself look at the sheriff's face and mutilated head once more. His own mother wouldn't know him . . . Working quickly, he put the cuffs on the sheriff and threw the key away.

With luck – maybe living up to his nickname for once – when the body was found they would think it was the prisoner who had drowned and been muti- lated by the river. Sooner or later they would find out the body showed signs of age that didn't fit Montana's description but by then he ought to be many miles away.

With a little luck. . . !

'And you claim your nickname isn't appropriate!'

Angie Bancroft said in the kitchen. They were eating their stew now and had been while Montana told his story. 'I'd say you had phenomonal luck, Mr Montana! *Good* luck.'

Gavin agreed.

'Never mind the "Mr Montana" – might as well call me "Lucky", I guess.'

'But how did you get way down here?' Gavin asked. 'Casper, Wyoming is a long way north.'

'I followed the river and came to a small town on the banks, stole a skiff and some grub, let the current take me. I was still pretty well tuckered out and I washed up somewhere south, awoke in the river one night, the skiff having overturned. Got ashore somehow, collapsed, and when I came to, heard cows and riders, saw a small ranch. Skirted around to where I could see the buildings, just a shack and a rope corral. Stole a horse but was seen and they chased me into the desert where they shot the horse from under me – and left me, with no food or water or even a gun. Next I know I woke up in a bough shelter and saw Claiborne and his pards working on Gavin. . . .'

They were silent, toying with what was left of their food now. Angie looked at Montana and he caught her eye. He smiled. 'OK – I really was lucky.'

'Lucky Montana. Perhaps I was lucky, too – that you turned up here when I need help so badly. Will you stay on? Help me fight off Rafferty?'

'I've seen him shoot, Sis,' Gavin added excitedly. 'We could sure use a man like him . . . what d'you say, Lucky?'

He sighed, looked from one to the other.
'Well, maybe my luck's changed for the better. Guess I might's well stick around and see.'

CHAPTER 6

GLOVES ARE OFF!

It was Montana who found Link Cady.

Lucky was riding the west boundary, familiarizing himself with the lay of Rafferty's land as much as that of A-Bar-W. The Irishman's spread ran mighty close in places, butting right up against an invisible 'line' so that it was anyone's guess where one ranch ended and the other began. Lucky Montana made a mental note to have Angie fence in this part. It would be too easy to accuse riders of trespassing and such accusations usually ended in a fight of some kind.

He spotted a couple of riders hitting the timber on a low knoll across on Rafferty's and shortly after caught a flash of sun on a lens. He smiled crookedly: they were watching him.

That was fine by him – it didn't bother Montana and he even waved once but the lens followed him.

Turning where the line seemed to deviate around a hogback – though it might have run right over it, splitting it down the middle – he would need to

check a survey map to be sure – he glimpsed movement on top of a lopside butte. He guessed by the
look of it that it was the one Gavin had pointed out
yesterday from another angle and told him was
called Broken Tooth. Without seeming to do so, he
watched the top as he rode but didn't see any more
movement. It might have been a cloud shadow, or a
gust of wind tipping the pale underside of brush
foliage to the sunlight. He veered away and headed
for country that started to rise. If he got high
enough, he could see better over onto Rafferty's side
– maybe flush the man with the glasses, too.

The ledge was weather-worn up here, with long
stretches of flat rock that angled down to a clearly
defined edge. Curious to see what lay beyond that
ledge, he rode across, the horse not keen to go too
close. So he dismounted, put a rock on the reins – he
didn't want to find himself afoot this far from the
ranch house if the animal decided to run off. He
wasn't sure why he took his rifle with him, old habits,
he supposed later, but he carried the Winchester
Angie had given him in his right hand as he
approached the edge, frowning when he saw scrape
marks in the shale leading to a broken section. He
could almost hear the iron horseshoes making those
marks as the animal was pulled reluctantly closer to
the edge.

He eased up a step at a time, and looked over. He
caught his breath – there was a drop of at least a
hundred feet onto a steep slope that ended in a
jumble of big rocks.

And lying among these was the carcass of a horse.

Some ten yards away and a little upslope was the body
of a man. Montana glanced up as a shadow passed
over him and he knew then what had caught his eye
up on the butte earlier: vultures gathering. Must've
seen him coming and perched along the edge of the
butte, patiently waiting for him to ride on. . . .

The horse was a piebald, one that Link Cady had
favoured, and when he thought about it he had seen
the cowboy riding out on it this morning right after
breakfast. In fact, he had tracked Link for a time
when he had come across a trail earlier and the sign
led him through brush-choked draws to a small
canyon where there were about forty cows penned in
by cut lodgepoles. There had been a small camp and
he had found a neckerchief he had seen Link wearing, crumpled it and put it in a saddle-bag.

He'd intended to ask Link some questions about
those mavericks when he saw him . . . He had left the
cattle where they were and continued on his ride. He
could see the river and the trail but there was no
further sign of Link. So he had kept on, ending up
here, looking on a crumpled body far below. There
would be no questions about any mavericks now.

He jumped as there was a puff of rock dust a foot
from his right boot swiftly followed by the whipcrack
of a rifle. Montana went down to one knee, twisting
so that he was facing back towards Broken Tooth
butte, rifle coming to his shoulder. He was exposed
here but he needed to get that damn bushwhacker's
head down before he made a run for cover.

His eagle eyes picked out the drifting gunsmoke
up there, allowed for the direction of the wind and

moved his rifle barrel slightly to his right. Another bullet ricocheted off the edge of the broken rock but he forced himself not to flinch, got off two fast hammering shots. Rock chips sprayed right underneath the new spurt of gunsmoke and he saw the blur as the hidden rifle lifted when the man threw himself backwards.

Montana was on his feet and running, crouched double, crossing the open stretch and zigzagging towards his horse which was standing with ears pricked, sniffing the hot mountain air. Lucky slapped at the reins as he ran past, clutching the strips of leather, dragging the startled mount's head around and in towards sheltering rocks. He vaulted into the saddle, paused briefly, then rowelled hard and with authority. The horse whinnied and its hind legs buckled for an instant before the shoes managed to get a grip on the shale, sparks flying.

He lunged the animal back the way he had come, racing it to where he had seen the movement on the high ground. Vultures wheeled high on the thermals, giving him a rough clue as to the ambusher's whereabouts. He set the horse at the steep slope, the animal stumbling and almost falling. As it did so, three bullets cut air around his body, one close enough to tug at the flapping corner of Walt Bancroft's soft leather vest that Angie had given him.

But he weaved the horse through the rocks and when he came into an open section, took the rein ends between his teeth, stood in the stirrups and brought the rifle up to his shoulder again. He raked the area up there where he knew the man to be, saw the flash of a grey shirt, a dark-coloured hat, before they disappeared behind a rock.

Montana settled back into the saddle, still holding the reins in his teeth as the animal grunted and heaved up the slope. He slipped cartridges from his belt loops and thumbed home four into the Winchester's loading gate.

Above the clatter and stertorous breathing of his mount, he heard the rattle of hoofs on rocks clearly – from above. He bared his teeth in a tight grin, sheathed the rifle now, took the reins in his hands and used them in concert with his knees and shifting weight, taking the struggling mount through the rocks, climbing all the time, using as much shelter as he could manage.

There was so long between gunfire from above that he was thinking maybe he had got in a lucky shot and hit the son of a bitch bad enough so he couldn't shoot. And hard on the thought came three hammering, booming shots, one of which almost took his head off as it sent his hat spinning.

Close! Much closer than he figured!

The killer was smarter than he had figured, too. He had quit the saddle, allowing his horse to run on riderless, waited until Montana came into view.

Lucky was leaving the horse in a headlong dive behind a rock that was almost a perfect sphere as he figured things out. He saw the patch of dirt and wrenched his body so that he landed on it, jarring and grunting. The man above shot down at him and bullets kicked dirt and whined off rocks all round him.

He had to stand up to get in a shot like that! Lucky thought and immediately slid around the curved base of his shelter, hesitated briefly, then stepped out into the open.

And there was the killer, standing on top of a rock, working his rifle lever as he aimed down into the small crevice where Montana had landed. He must have seen Lucky out of the corner of his eye and spun swiftly, rifle coming round.

Montana, crouching, fired with the butt against his hip, two fast shots that spurted dust from the killer's shirt and knocked the man flailing from his perch. The body hit hard, leg jammed between two rocks, the smoking rifle clattering. Montana levered in a fresh shell, went in warily, soon stood over the unmoving man. He saw by the smashed mouth and general violent rearrangement of the man's face that it was McColl, the man he had hit with the sapling, full force, out at Midget Mountain that day. . . .

McColl was dead.

'You're trespassing, feller,' Montana told him quietly. 'A long way into A-Bar-W land here – and the only reason I can think of that brought you here was to push Link Cady and his horse off the rim.'

There was blood on McColl's hands and shirt front, dried blood, smeared, like a man would get carrying something or someone already dead or nearly so, having been badly beaten first.

The fresh bullet wounds Lucky had given him hadn't bled much because they had both been right smack through the middle of the man's heart, stopping it instantly.

*

Angie Bancroft, watching through the parlour window, gasped and put a hand to her mouth as she watched the rider coming into the yard, a travois dragging behind his weary mount, a bundle of bloody rags resting between the splayed poles.

Instinctively, she knew whoever it was on that *travois* was dead. . . .

She called Gavin and together they went outside and met Montana as he dismounted wearily.

'It's Link. Someone – I think McColl – beat him and then pushed him over a cliff near Broken Tooth, with his piebald, trying to make it look like an accident.'

Palefaced, Angie whispered, 'Just like Walt's. . . .'

They had questions, of course, but Angie could see how his ride had taken its toll, got him seated on the small porch and brought him a glass of fresh lemonade. He drank, nodded his thanks, then told them about the gunfight with McColl.

'You nearly caught him at it, eh?' Gavin asked but Lucky didn't seem too sure.

'Saw two men riding into some brush and one of them put field-glasses on me soon afterward. The sun kept flashing off the lens – and I figured he was mighty careless, but I think he wanted to hold my attention while the other one – McColl – slipped back across the river and tried to bushwhack me. Reckon they were on their way back after throwing Link off that cliff.'

Gavin nodded to the *travois* where old Horseshoe

had now come to look at what it held. 'What makes you think Link was beaten first? I mean, there's not too much left to see.'

'Gavin!' Angie said sharply but Lucky said, 'He's got bruises on his side – in the shape of a riding boot. Ribs are all stove-in, of course, but there's a big bruise on his belly – I've seen enough men stomped half to death to recognize a boot-heel's mark. . . .'

'That's enough!' Angie was white-faced, worried. 'D'you think McColl, and whoever was riding with him—'

'Would've been Lindsey,' Gavin put in tightly. 'They always stick together.

'Whoever it was,' Angie continued, 'd'you think they beat Link, Lucky?'

'Be my guess, but he needn't have been beat-up on your land. Could've dragged him across earlier and done it on Rafferty's place, then tried to make it look like an accident when they went too far. '

'I believe it was probably Claiborne,' she said quietly, hands clasped tightly. 'He's beaten men badly before this. Other ranchers who didn't want to sell had cowhands beaten and driven off or were sometimes attacked themselves by Claiborne . . . but why Link?'

'You just said it, Sis – you don't want to sell, so they beat him and probably told him to clear the valley, but it was too late so . . .' He shrugged, nodded towards the *travois*.

'Or they might've been trying to find out something about me.'

They looked sharply at Montana.

76

'I'm the mystery man. They must be wondering if you'd sent for me, Angie.'

'Sent for you? Why?'

'Hired a hardcase for fighting pay.' Montana saw her face straighten as she thought about this.

She put a hand to her mouth. 'My God! If Rafferty thinks that, he'll believe I'm ready to fight, I mean, really *fight* him!' Looking shaken, she sat down slowly on the stoop. 'Who knows what he'll do? As long as I just refused his offers to buy, I didn't believe he would do too much to hassle me. . . .'

'You don't know that, Sis! Look what happened to Billy Shumaker? They burned him out, his eldest son was shot and might never walk again – and Halliday always claimed that it was Rafferty's men who drove his herd off Bison Butte. Killed two hundred prime beeves and left him stony broke.'

'So Rafferty knows how to play rough. . . .'

She sighed, staring into space. 'Nothing was ever proved – but then that's not surprising with a sheriff like Windy Nichols investigating.' She looked at Montana. 'It seems to me, Lucky, that now the gloves are off.'

He nodded. 'Glad you see that. No use me riding out, not now they've killed Link. They won't stop; can't afford to now they've tipped their hand. Angie, we're gonna have to get ready for a range war.'

She tightened at his words, looked from Montana to Gavin to Old Horseshoe as he limped up towards the porch.

This was her crew – all she had to stand between her and Rafferty.

She shivered, felt instinctively that it wasn't enough and that if Sean Rafferty went all-out – well, she would lose A-Bar-W.

CHAPTER 7

'WHO IS HE?'

Sheriff Windy Nichols was dozing in his chair, head thrown back, tonsils rattling as he snored, boots up on the desk.

Rafferty and Claiborne entered and banged on the edge of the desk but the lawman snored on. The rancher nodded and Claiborne swept Nichols' boots off the desk. They slammed down to the floor with a thud, jarring the lawman awake, a curse on his lips as he fought to stay in his chair, grabbing an arm as it swivelled, glaring at his visitors.

His face straightened abruptly and he leapt awkwardly to his feet when he recognized Sean Rafferty.

'Ah – howdy, Sean. Just catchin' up on a bit of shut-eye. Busy night last night.'

'No wonder you find it hard to sleep at night when you sleep all day, Sheriff,' the rancher said sardonically. He flicked a kerchief at the straightback chair opposite the desk and sat down slowly, folded his hands over the silver top of his ebony cane.

Claiborne leaned a beefy shoulder against the wall near the gun cabinet, rugged face unsmiling.

Nichols ran a hand around his jaw and the day-old stubble rasped. 'I looked into McColl's shootin', like you asked, Sean, but I couldn't find anything worthwhile.' He lowered his voice conspiratorily. 'Less'n you count his tracks were well into A-Bar-W land. I'd say that's where he was shot but – what the hell was he doin' trespassin' so far onto Angie's place?'

'Forget McColl – he had plenty of enemies, and I *know* that this new man of Angie's was one of them. Lindsey's pretty sure he killed Mac but there's no way to prove it.'

'Well, whoever it was nailed him dead centre through the ticker.'

'Link said this Lucky was a dead-shot,' Claiborne allowed, but neither man took any notice of him.

'What've you found out so far?' Rafferty asked Nichols and the sheriff looked mighty uncomfortable.

'Hardly anythin', Sean – look, you gotta unnerstan' that I ain't got much to go on. Feller's found staggerin' in the desert, says he's got no memory of bein' there – I mean, how can I say different?'

Rafferty sighed, leaned forward a little. 'We know now that he came down from the north, a long way north according to Link. You send some telegrams to lawmen up that way, far as Montana if you have to. Ask about anyone wanted using the nickname of "Lucky" and anything they've got on him – is that so hard?'

Nichols shrugged and took a cheroot from a vest pocket and lit up. 'Ain't hard, Sean, but it's costly—'

Rafferty flicked his gaze to Claiborne who moved swiftly and kicked the chair Nichols sat in. It spun wildly, Nichols grabbing at the arm, shouting 'Hey!' and then Claiborne stopped it abruptly and the sheriff slid off the seat, scrabbled wildly to keep from sprawling on the floor.

'God-damn! What the hell you doin', Clay?'

'Mr Rafferty pays you plenty! So just *send the goddamn telegraphs*!' Claiborne grabbed his shirt front and thumped him down into his chair. The burning cheroot fell into the sheriff's lap and he scrabbled wildly for it, picked it up, burning his fingers. Claiborne snatched it from him and rammed the burning end against the lawman's ear.

Windy Nichols screamed and writhed, doubled up as he clapped a hand to his stinging ear, obviously scared now.

Nichols looked up at Rafferty, tears of pain in his eyes. 'Judas, Sean, I done what you asked! I sent heaps of telegraphs. . . .'

'To all the wrong places,' Rafferty told him calmly. 'Now you send 'em north this time – and you find out who this son of a bitch *is*! I want an answer in two days. If I don't get one, Clay here will come visit you. . . .'

'Aw, no need for that, Sean.'

Rafferty stood. 'I hope not. Now get on to it, Windy. Two days maximum.'

They left then and Nichols dropped back into his chair, still muttering curses as he wet his fingers with spittle and rubbed it on his burning earlobe. He felt a stir of cold hatred but swiftly put it down. He knew he would never do anything about the anger and resentment he felt for Rafferty and that snake, Claiborne.

Instead, he took out a ledger from his desk and began searching for the names of lawmen in the far north, his hand shaking noticeably.

Rafferty and Claiborne were walking towards the livery where they had left their mounts when the ramrod suddenly stopped, reaching out a hand to grab his boss's arm, stopping the rancher in mid-stride and earning him a glowering look.

'Chief! There he is! Goddamnit – there he *is*!'

Rafferty recognized Lucky Montana from his visit to Angie's.

He was just coming out of the general store with young Gavin Leach, each man carrying a gunnysack of supplies towards mounts tethered at the hitch rail.

'Time we found out just how good this feller is, ain't it, chief?' Claiborne asked tightly. His eyes narrowed as he watched Angie's men tie their sacks on the horses. 'I mean, he blind-sided me once, took us by surprise with a damn shotgun which I still figure likely wasn't even loaded – wonder how good he is in a square-off.'

'No gunplay, Clay – not just yet.' Rafferty said quickly. 'Remember Mac – it had to've been Lucky who killed him. The kid couldn't do it, Link was out of it, and that only leaves Horseshoe or the girl. It had to've been Lucky.'

'Just another reason to brace him, chief! What d'you say?'

Rafferty hesitated: violent confrontation wasn't his style at this stage of the game, or unless he was forced into it. But Claiborne had a legitimate beef with this man. It would look OK, and test them both – and those damn investors *were* crowding him; he needed to show them he was doing *something.* . . .

'I hope you're up to it, Clay!' he said finally.

Claiborne snorted and spat in the dust, hitching at his trouser belt. 'Send someone for the sawbones, Chief – Lucky's "luck" is about to run out.'

He was moving away with long strides before he even finished speaking and when only a few yards from Montana and Gavin, the young greenhorn spotted Claiborne, swiftly spoke a warning to his companion.

'Trouble!'

Lucky looked up casually, tightened his rope on the grubsack and turned to face the storming Claiborne, looking at his ease.

'I want to talk to you!' gritted Claiborne, still striding in fast.

'No you don't,' Montana replied. 'What you want to do is beat my head in – or try to. See how you go.'

And Gavin Leach gasped as Montana stepped forward, weaved to one side and drove a fist into Claiborne's midriff.

The Rafferty ramrod grunted and doubled up, sliding back a pace or two. Montana followed, lifted a knee into his face and when he straightened slammed two left jabs into his face, hooked with a right and knocked Claiborne off the boardwalk to flounder in the street. He stepped down as Claiborne shook his head and instinctively fought to his feet.

Montana stepped forward to slam him again but his ankle turned in a rain-eroded gutter and he stumbled. His blow passed over Claiborne's right shoulder and the man lunged forward, getting the point of his left shoulder into Montana's mid-section. Lucky grunted and grabbed at the man's thick body as the ramrod's weight carried him back and down.

They rolled and kicked and elbowed and punched and snarled as they fought to get their feet under them. The horses at the hitch rack whinnied and shied and stomped and Claiborne yelled as a hoof gouged his riding boot. Lucky got a knee into the man's chest, heaved him away, rolled to hands and knees and jumped upright.

The Rafferty ramrod was only a second behind him and they met again with boots dug in, hips swivelling as they traded blow after blow, skin tearing, blood splashing. Lucky threw up a left forearm, parrying a blow, but it was a feint and Clay got him with his other fist alongside the jaw. Montana's head snapped sideways and he staggered. Claiborne bulled in, fists cocked, then hammering, his sheer weight driving Montana backwards. Then Lucky stopped, stepped nimbly to the left, twisting side-on at the same time. Claiborne stumbled with the force of the blow he had swung and Lucky clipped him on the ear, moved around and hooked him twice in the ribs, each blow bringing a loud grunt of pain from the other, Clay's feet leaving the ground. Then

Montana drove a straight right with his shoulder behind it into Claiborne's face, but it was a little off and didn't finish the fight as Lucky had expected.

The ramrod floundered, dodged a boot, and thrust up like a piston rising in a steam cylinder, met Lucky's charge with legs braced. Montana staggered back as he met the solid wall of muscle and flesh. Claiborne sniffed, wiped the back of a hand across his bleeding nose – and that habit, only a second or two – cost him a punch under the left eye that sent him reeling, his neck feeling as if it had snapped.

His arms flayed at the air and he spun in a kind of macabre dance, and when he got his balance, Lucky Montana was waiting with cocked fists. They hammered Clay from jaw to brisket, Montana's elbows working, fists blurring as they bruised ribs and solar plexus. Claibourne clutched at his assailant, trying to stay on his feet. His legs were caving in and Lucky stepped back. Claiborne reached desperately, fell forward – right onto a rising knee.

He went down hard and was slow to attempt getting up this time, the world swimming dizzily around him. Lucky, breathing hard, face smeared with blood, stepped forward, and drove a boot into Clay's side.

The man rolled over, drawing up his knees. Montana towered above him, nudged him roughly with a boot toe, and when the sick ramrod made no attempt to rise, reached down and twisted his fingers in the long greasy hair.

Claiborne yelled as he was lifted, feeling as if his scalp was tearing away. He thrashed and flailed but

85

when his head was just above Montana's waist level, Lucky said, 'Link sent this!'

And drove a clubbed fist down into that ugly, bloody face. Folk who had gathered to watch heard the nose go and the teeth *clunk* together hard enough to break, or at least chip. A dreadful shudder passed clear through Claiborne's entire body and his eyes rolled up, showing the whites. Lucky hit him again, between the eyes, and let him go.

Rafferty's ramrod fell face first into the dust, no more fight left in him.

Lucky Montana stood there, swaying on rubbery legs, breathing hard, chest heaving as he fumbled for a kerchief and dabbed at his bloody face. Then he felt Gavin Leach leading him to the horse trough and the gaping spectators opened out to let them through.

It was quite a spectacle to see a man like Claiborne spread out in the dust, beaten down and bloody.

After sluicing water on his face, Montana looked up and saw Rafferty standing on the walk. He tossed the Irishman a mocking salute.

'You'll need better men than that,' he panted, but Rafferty showed no reaction, merely turned and spoke to Sheriff Nichols who had come running up, carrying a sawn-off shotgun down at his side. The rancher paid no attention to his battered foreman as someone dragged Clay over to the walk clear of the traffic. The man groaned as he started to come to slowly – and mighty painfully. But Rafferty pointed to Lucky Montana and snapped at the lawman.

'Arrest that man! He started the fight – I sent Clay

across to tell him I'd like a word and next thing he's beating on him!'

Plenty in the crowd murmured – a lot of people had seen how the fight started and they were on Montana's side. Many of them had felt Claiborne's bullying fists over the years. Nichols licked his lips, but at a savage glare from Rafferty he stepped down and started towards Montana.

'I want a word with you about the shootin' of McColl anyways, mister!' the sheriff said, bringing the shotgun up into both hands, a thumb poised over a hammer.

'Save your breath, Sheriff,' Lucky said, still breathing a little hard. 'McColl laid for me at Broken Tooth, bushwhacked me.' He held out the punctured corner of the leather vest and showed the bullet hole. 'If someone'll hand me my hat, I'll show you a hole in the brim – fired from above. I can take you to the place, show you fresh bullet marks on rocks, all from above where McColl lay. I can show you his boot prints on the edge of the cliff above where I found Link Cady and his horse amongst the rocks below.'

Nichols blinked. 'You sayin' Mac pushed Link off?'

Lucky shook his head. 'No – I'm saying he *threw* him off, his body, leastways. Because Claiborne had already beat him to death. They were trying to make it look like an accident, just as they did with Walt Bancroft, but he spotted me riding in and decided to square a couple things he figured he owed me.'

'This man's crazy,' Rafferty said easily. 'You'd do everyone a favour by locking him up and checking his background, Sheriff.'

Montana set his hard gaze on the rancher. 'Take a look at Claiborne's boots. Splashed with brown marks – it's Link Cady's dried blood. I found boot-marks on Link's ribs. Check Clay's trousers, too. They're splashed with more blood, not from the fight, but a long time before when he beat up on Link.'

Nichols was bewildered but Rafferty's bleak gaze told him what to do. He moved the ball of his thumb swiftly to the spur of the gun hammer, aiming to cock the weapon.

There was the crash of a gunshot that scattered the crowd and made Rafferty leap for his life as the shot-gun spun from Nichols' grip and the sheriff yelped, grabbed at his numbed fingers and stared at the bullet burn across the back of his hand. He snapped his gaze up fearfully and saw the smoking six-gun braced against Lucky Montana's hip.

Gavin Leach, white-faced, stood about a yard away, staring. The crowd gaped and Claiborne, half-conscious, let his aching, swollen jaw drop a couple of inches.

'Sheriff,' Montana said slowly, 'you've got no reason to arrest me. I don't aim to let you arrest me. You try again and maybe my next bullet'll do more than just tear a gun outa your hands.'

'I-I can charge you with attempted murder, resistin' lawful arrest, woundin' a lawman. . . .' blustered Nichols but paused when Lucky merely shook his head slowly.

'You can do those things, Sheriff, but only if you

want to die. And you don't look to me like the kinda lawman who's willing to lay his life on the line.'

Nichols swallowed and Rafferty snorted in disgust and strode away angrily towards the livery. The sheriff, wrapping a kerchief around his bleeding hand, started after him.

'Wait up, Mr Rafferty! I-I cain't do nothin'! You seen him! Half-brother to a bolt of lightnin'!'

'Get those telegraphs away!' Rafferty snapped, entering the livery.

By that time, Gavin and Montana were riding slowly out of town towards the A Bar W trail.

'You're in plenty of trouble now,' Gavin opined,

'Been in worse.'

'But – you wounded a lawman!'

'He's not a lawman: he's Rafferty's man.'

Gavin stared a while. 'I've never met anyone like you, Lucky.'

'We're a dying breed. Oops! Mebbe I could've worded that better.' Lucky winced, putting a hand swiftly up against his aching jaw. 'That Claiborne packs a wallop.'

'Yes, he's a tough customer, all right. But did you need to hit him that last time?' Gavin asked tautly, and Montana looked at him through a puffed eye on that side.

'Why not?'

'Well, he was already beat. Seemed unnecessary to me.'

'Now he'll remember it – new experience for him.'

After a dozen more paces, the kid said, 'Why'd you say that about Link? "This one's for Link!" I mean, he wasn't much of a man and you didn't seem to take to him.'

'He worked for Angie, didn't he? Took his beating while on her payroll.'

'Ye-es, but he was obviously going to steal from her – I mean, those mavericks you found hidden away.'

Montana hitched slightly in the saddle, unnerved the kid the way he looked at him out of that battered, still bleeding face.

'Kid, you've got a lot to learn. A man don't have to be a saint seven ways to Sunday just because he rides for the same brand – what matters is, good or bad, if he rides alongside you, he's your pard for the time being and if anything happens to him, the same thing could happen to you. So you fight – on his behalf as much as yours. You fight for the brand and whoever rides for it, no matter whether you like 'em or not.'

Gavin flushed, then said, 'I never expected to hear that kind of philosphy from a – an admitted outlaw!'

Montana smiled faintly and it was obvious it hurt to do it.

'Like I said, kid, you've still got a lot to learn.'

CHAPTER 8

GUNSLINGER

Angie Bancroft wasn't pleased with the news.

'That was rather extreme, wasn't it, drawing your gun on a lawman, whether he's straight or crooked?'

Montana arched his eyebrows. 'He was cocking the hammer on a shotgun.'

'And Lucky beat him!' Gavin put in, unable to keep the excitement from his voice. 'I couldn't believe it. Half the town was there and they couldn't believe it either! He drew and fired while Nichols was still cocking the hammer – and the sheriff wasn't doing it in slow motion.'

Angie frowned. 'You have a reputation as – as a gunslinger?' she asked Montana.

He shrugged. 'Up north a few might've heard of me – small frog in a big pond. There're others faster.'

'I'd sure like to see 'em!' Gavin said, with a sceptical chuckle.

Montana was sober. 'There's a man named Dawson. . . .'

'The man your enemies hired . . . ?' Angie said slowly.

He nodded. 'Hell in a hand-basket with a six-gun.'

'Is he still looking for you?'

'Guess so. They say once he takes a job he don't quit till it's finished – even when the hire money runs out, he's been known to keep on till he gets his man.'

Her frown deepened. 'Then he could trail you here?'

Lucky hesitated. 'Doubt it. That dead sheriff I put the handcuffs on ought to hold things for a while. If you want me to move on, Angie, say so. Don't be afraid to speak up.'

She tossed her head, met his gaze steadily. 'I won't. I just hope you haven't brought a lot of trouble down on yourself, and indirectly A Bar W, by shooting at Windy Nichols.'

'If I have, I'll handle it – and keep you out of it.'

'You told me a man rides and fights for the brand he works for,' Gavin said slowly. 'Shouldn't that work the other way round, too?'

Lucky smiled slowly: his injuries felt a little better since Angie had doctored them with iodine and arnica. 'I'd like to think so, kid, but sometimes it's easier and wiser for a rancher to disown some troublemaker she's hired.'

Angie looked indignant. 'That's not the case here! I hired you to help me keep this ranch. Any trouble you find yourself in is my trouble, too, and you can rely on the fact that I'll back you to the hilt.'

Montana nodded briefly, hitched at his gunbelt. 'Well we all seem to know what we ought to do, so what's next, Angie?'

'I was thinking maybe you had a suggestion? I mean, I don't want to carry this fight to Rafferty and give him reason to use Nichols and his version of the law against us, or an excuse to call in a crew on fighting wages.'

She and Gavin both looked expectantly at Lucky Montana.

'I think we should let things lie for now. I'll take a ride through the valley, have a talk with the few spreads you told me still remain.'

'Only because they're on the fringe, or up too high for Rafferty to bother with, but there are still a couple of the ranchers who sold out to him under pressure living on their places until he's ready to flood the valley. He agreed to that.'

'OK, I'll go see 'em. Give me a week, maybe. That'll keep Nichols off your back if I'm not here, anyway.'

Gavin looked alarmed. 'What if Rafferty makes a move?'

'He won't – he's not sure of me yet. He thinks I could be a drifter, looking to hire out my gun, an outlaw on the run, maybe even undercover law. Because he's up to something that's not as legal as he tries to make it appear.'

Angie looked puzzled. 'What gives you that idea? It seems legal enough, buying our ranches, his scheme backed by businessmen back East – and the government, he claims.'

'Not sure the government's in it right now. It'll help, I guess, if he comes up with an acceptable plan.

93

The men who control the public pursestrings usually want ironclad guarantees before they invest a dollar. As for "businessmen", they're in it for profit and won't look too closely at his methods. I think he'll sit tight till he's sure I'm not any real threat to him, just someone on your payroll, Angie.'

'I hope you're right.' She looked worried now.

He smiled crookedly. 'I think Rafferty knows enough about me already to be leery. Heard him tell Nichols to send off some telegraphs as he went into the livery. Reckon they'll be to check up on me. It'll take a week at least for him to get all replies and I'll be back here by then.'

As he stood to leave, setting his bullet-clipped hat squarely on his head, she moved in and placed a hand on his forearm, looking up into his battered face.

'Take care, Lucky. Try and live up to your nick-name.'

'Do my best. Gav, you want to get me a sack of grub and some spare ammo?'

At the corral, while Montana was finishing saddling his claybank, Gavin brought out the food and ammunition. He tied them on behind the cantle and asked, 'Those replies to Nichols' wires, Lucky – just the way you said about it taking a week, made me think that maybe Nichols or Rafferty could expect something about you they might not want to hear. . . .'

Montana stepped up into the saddle, grunting a little with small stabs of pain from his bruises and stiff joints.

'Whatever they hear they won't like, kid – guarantee that.'

He nodded, wheeled the horse and rode off across the sun-hammered pastures towards the hills.

Young Gavin pursed his lips thoughtfully, then, as Angie came out onto the porch with a bowl of peas to shell, he called, 'Sis, I'm going riding – think I'll have a bit more practice with my guns.' As her head snapped up at his words, he added, 'No use kidding ourselves, sis, it's going to get down to shooting any time now . . . I have to be ready.'

She knew he was right. Her heart beat faster, and she felt afraid, but she couldn't find the words to stop him.

The first rancher met Lucky with a rifle, standing in the doorway of the small shack not far from the banks of the Viper River. He looked work-worn and tired, his clothes patched, hair straggly, and he was unshaven. There was movement behind him in the shack and Lucky heard a child's voice, whining for something, a woman remonstrating.

'That's far enough, mister.' The man lifted the rifle and squinted as Montana halted the claybank and leaned his crossed hands on the saddlehorn in the universal sign that he had no hostile intentions. The man ran his eyes over the silent Montana. 'You look like a gunslinger to me.'

Lucky straightened in the saddle, the movement making the rancher tense. 'Relax, *amigo*, I'm not a Rafferty man.'

'You say – what d'you want?'

'Just come to see how you're getting on. Rafferty give you a deadline?'

The man squinted again, moved his rifle to a better position for shooting. 'Deadline? Well, he said we could stay on till he's ready to flood. Dunno when that is.'

'You get your money?'

'Not yet.' The man was tightening up and Lucky watched him warily: a nervous man with a cocked gun pointing at you wasn't anything to take casually. 'We stayed because we got nowheres else to go till he pays up.'

'When did he say he'd do that?'

'You ask a lot of questions, stranger.'

'Bad habit of mine. Name's Lucky Montana.'

It meant nothing to the rancher who said his name was McGovern. 'Why you want to know these things?'

'Working for Angie Bancroft. Had a few run-ins with Rafferty and Claiborne. Like to know all I can about a man who's after my hide.'

McGovern studied him more closely. 'A drunk went through here late at night, whoopin' and a'hollerin'. I come out to tell him to shut up and he said he just had to let everyone in the valley know he'd seen Claiborne hammered into the dust on Main Street – that wouldn'ta been you done it, would it?'

'Aw shucks,' Montana said, putting on an exaggerated bashful look, smiling at the same time.

The rancher snorted. 'My God! Listen, we ain't got much, but you're welcome to anythin' we have. That Claiborne son of a bitch beat my two cowhands silly and made threats agin Nan and the kids – it's why I agreed to sell. You gotta tell me what you done to that hardcase bastard.'

'Not much to tell, but I'll trade it for whatever you can give me by way of information.'

'Done deal, pard – you step on down and come in.'

He lowered the gun and stood to one side of the door. Montana swung down easily and doffed his hat as he entered the draughty shack.

The next place along had three tough-looking *hombres* working on it, removing heavy, Eastern-made furniture from the log house and stacking it on a couple of Conestoga covered wagons. Their mounts wore the Rafferty brand.

The one who came to meet Montana as he rode in slowly didn't have a gun in his hand, but he wore his six-gun tied down and kept a hand on the butt as he spat a stream of tobacco juice, looking up at the rider. His two companions went on bringing out furniture.

'You're trespassin', mister, Mr Rafferty owns this place now.' He was broad and muscular but not more than mediumn height and his eyes were restless, never staying on Lucky's face more than a few seconds.

'Where're the folk who built this place?'

'Who knows? Who cares? They've gone, and Mr Rafferty said to take the furniture they left as part of the deal. Now I've told you more'n you need to know. Turn round and ride on out.'

'Looks like good quality furniture,' Montana remarked as he watched the other two struggle to load a heavy mahogany sideboy with carved front and doors. 'Like the stuff they'd brought out with 'em when they migrated.'

'So? They were immigrants, couldn't make a go of it. Mr Rafferty gave 'em a good price.'

'Good for him, but what about the immigrants?'

The man stepped back, his hand tightening on the gun butt. 'I told you to vamoose!'

'Heard you. This was the Higgins place, wasn't it? The husband had some kind of a fall he never really spoke much about – busted both his legs. And his two men quit on him after being beaten up in a staged bar-room brawl. No wonder he couldn't make a go of it.'

'Been talkin' to that gossipin' McGovern, ain't you?' The broad man whistled shrilly once, not turning, and the other two stopped their work and came striding across. They were cut from the same mould as the man who faced Montana. 'Told this sonuver to move along twice – don't seem to want to do it. Guess we'll have to help him. . . .'

He jerked his head towards Montana and the two men lunged at the horse. Lucky rowelled the claybank abruptly and it whickered as it leapt forward. The startled men jumped aside and Montana leaned from the saddle, kicked one in the neck and knocked him sprawling, yanked the horse's head around violently as the other man grabbed for the bridle.

The claybank's head smashed into the man and he stumbled back, both hands going up to his face.

Blood ran between the fingers as his legs gave way and he sat down, dazed.

The broad man lifted his six-gun in a fast movement, but it was Montana's Colt that roared and he yelled, floundered as he dropped his gun and clutched at his bleeding arm. Lucky jumped the horse into him, knocking him flat, allowed the animal to step on him, the man screaming now.

Montana wheeled the horse, smoking gun still in his hand. He looked down coldly at the three floundering men.

'You'd be wise to cart that furniture into town. The Higginses are staying with her sister in a cabin on the north side, much too damn small . . . like McGovern, they're waiting for Rafferty to square-up what he owes 'em. You give 'em their furniture and they'll be able to afford to rent a decent place until he pays 'em. McGovern says Mrs Higgins is expecting. Got all that? Because I'll check it's done.'

It was the man who had greeted him who spoke, biting back the pain from his bullet-burned arm. 'Rafferty'll kill us.'

'He doesn't, I will,' Montana said, without expression and rode on out, leaving them staring after him.

The one who had been kicked in the neck could hardly speak but he rasped, 'Hell with this – I'm ridin' out.'

'Me, too,' said the man whose face had been mangled by the horse's swinging head.

The broad man staggered to his feet, face tight with pain. 'You ain't goin' nowhere – not till we deliver this load to the Higginses – then I'll come with you. I ain't gonna be the one to stay behind and tell Rafferty what happened.' He looked after Lucky Montana riding out along the river by now. 'That son of a bitch is a gunslinger if ever I seen one and Rafferty ain't payin' us no fightin' wages. . . .'

Angie Bancroft had more than 200 head of cattle grazing free in her river pasture.

The majority of them had been mavericks that her husband and the cowhands they had hired had rounded-up in the hills, brought down to the river grass and branded them with the A Bar W. They had wintered well there and now with spring moving along nicely after a little rain, the grass was lush and the cows were packing on the beef.

By the time summer was here they would be ready for driving to the railhead and shipping to the meat houses. She was looking forward to getting a good price because her herd had come down from the hills earlier than others in the valley and she hoped her trail drive would be first out of the valley. Besides, there were no other herds worthy of the name ready for the drive to railhead, not now Rafferty was buying out everyone. As for Rafferty's own herds, well, he would move them at any time, bullying his way up-valley, letting his cows feed on the grass of the small ranches, promising to pay once his beef was sold, but never doing it.

Angie hoped Lucky Montana would still be here when trail-drive time came around. She had a feeling that this year she was going to need all the help she could get.

And a man like Montana, with his guns, was just what the doctor ordered. . . .

But Angie needn't have worried about the coming trail drive. For two nights after Lucky had started his ride through the Viper River Valley, a small band of dark riders crossed the river from the direction of Rafferty's and paused at the barbed wire fence that kept the cattle from wandering into the river.

'Remember, don't cut the wire,' a muffled voice said quietly. 'Work on the posts, snap 'em off at ground level, or pull 'em out. When the wire slacks off, lay it on the ground or as close as it'll go. . . .'

There were four men and they were all masked with bandannas covering the lower halves of their faces. The cows were scattered through the pasture, not needing nighthawks, being a small herd in a fenced section of lush grass. They were content and wouldn't wander far. The fence was there just to make sure.

The riders tore it down along the river side of the pasture, set their horses across and then rode in on the sleeping cows. They had smoke pots with them, a mixture of gunpowder and greasy rags with short fuses, in old preserve jars.

At a word from the leader, matches flared and fuses spluttered and the pots were hurled amongst the bunches of cattle. The powder flashed without exploding, but it hissed and crackled and made the pots jump as if they were living things, flaring brightly, terrifyingly. Some hit the cows and the beasts bawled as hide singed and burning powder spattered them, smoke stinging eyes and rasping at nostrils.

The men rode around the frantic cows, pushing

them into several small bunches, then driving them together into one large bunch.

By now they were hard to control and the flares were dying, but a pall of thick smoke hung like a curtain between them and the house so they turned towards the only way out – over and through the sagging fence and into the river.

There were men waiting on the far bank, riding out into the water, turning back the first of the swimming, eye-rolling, bawling cows that tried to make it to Rafferty land.

The other men were crowding them from behind and the two lots met and mixed it up, shoulder to shoulder, horns gouging, panicked steers leaping on top of others, cloven hoofs tearing flesh and bringing more pain and more panic.

The river churned as the cows battled each other and the riders, churned and foamed until the muddy waters took on a reddish hue, the colour visible even on this moonless night.

The men crossed upstream from the drowning chaos, met with the others, and rode back to the Rafferty bunkhouse, only two staying behind to wipe out their tracks and collect the remains of the smoke pots from the trampled pasture.

They were gone by the time lights showed in the distant house, the blood-chilling bawling of the steers finally loud enough to rouse the inhabitants.

A little while later, gunshots crackled through the night along the river as crippled steers were put out of their misery and Angie and Gavin began to count their losses.

Even Old Horseshoe limped down to help, bringing a battered pot of his infamous coffee and a couple of tin cups.

But even that powerful brew failed to settle Angie's nerves.

She had been counting on that herd to see her through, the money helping her to fend off Rafferty.

Without it she knew she would go under.

CHAPTER 9

BUSHWHACKED

Angie and Gavin stood on the river-bank, smoking rifles down at their sides, old Horsehoe standing in the background with his battered black coffee pot.

'It was Rafferty,' Gavin said tightly.

Angie glanced at him sharply: she knew it had to be connected to Sean Rafferty in some way but she didn't care for the kid's sudden cold tone or the unaccustomed hard look in his eyes. As he spoke and surveyed the slaughter, he was pushing fresh cartridges through the loading gate of the hot rifle. He rested it against a rock, took out his Colt and checked the loads in the cylinder.

'We can't go off half-cocked on this, Gavin,' she said quickly. 'If we make any kind of move against Rafferty he'll use Windy Nichols to cause us no end of trouble, maybe throw us in jail – and in no time at all he'd have his hands on A Bar W.'

'Like hell he will!' There it was again, that bleakness in his face and voice, like she had seen and heard in Lucky Montana when he had braced

Rafferty and his men that time with the unloaded shotgun. 'There's broken glass all over the pasture, blackened patches – Horseshoe said they're from smoke pots.'

Angie looked levelly at the old cook. 'Smoke pots. . . ?'

'Some call 'em flash pots,' Horseshoe told her. 'Pack a preserve jar with some gunpowder and ram greasy rags on top. Set it off with a fuse of just a strip of burnin' rag and toss 'em in among a herd. They flash, smoke like crazy, but there's no bang. Scare the cows outa their hides. We used it in the army to stampede Injun ponies before we hit their camp.'

Angie had seen the snapped-off fence posts and had at first believed it was a stampede set off by some natural force that had terrified the herd. But she had wondered about those streaked black flowers on the ground in several places. . . .

'Gavin!' she snapped suddenly, aware that her brother was running towards his horse, ground-hitched ten yards back. 'What're you doing?'

'Going to brace Rafferty, Sis. This is my fault. I should've been riding nighthawk and it wouldn't've happened.'

'You little fool! If you had been, you'd be dead now!' She started to run after him but Gavin was already jumping into the saddle, ramming his rifle home in the scabbard, rein ends between his teeth as he did so, using his knees to turn his horse. 'Gavin! Please! Don't. . . .'

'I'm going to have it out with Rafferty once and for all! I'll be back, Sis!

105

He splashed the mount into the river and urged it across, the noise of the river drowning his sister's screamed words.

He disappeared into the brush on the other side rowelling his horse brutally, heading fast into Rafferty land.

She rounded on Horseshoe. 'Why didn't you stop him!' she shouted unfairly, but the old man sniffed and shrugged.

'Kid's got the right notions, Angie. You can thank Lucky Montana for that.'

'To hell with Lucky Montana! I could kill him for planting such notions in Gavin's head!' Tears flooded suddenly. Her voice broke. 'He – he'll be killed! He's still only a boy, Horseshoe! He thinks because he can shoot pretty good – that – that he can—'

'I can still ride,' cut in Horseshoe abruptly. 'You just gimme a boost up into your saddle, Angie, and gimme that rifle. I'll catch up with Gav.'

'I-I can't let you do that, Horseshoe – you—'

'Angie, I'm the best one, the only one to go after him.' He snatched the rifle from her suddenly and stepped up onto a rock beside her tethered horse, balancing on his good leg. 'You gonna gimme me a boost or do I do it myself? Gav's gettin' closer to Rafferty all the time.'

Crying with anger and frustration and outright fear, Angie helped settle the oldster into the saddle. She jumped back as he kicked the horse away with his good foot and turned it towards the river.

'Horseshoe! Be careful!' she called after him, as

106

he rode into the river. 'Bring him back safely – and you, too.'

Gavin rode much faster than Horsehoe – he didn't even know the oldster was behind him. He pulled ahead, weaving his mount through dry washes and draws, unfamiliar with Rafferty's land. He rode into several dead ends, wheeled around, swearing, disori-ented, and, after the fourth time, felt his belly knot as he saw a rider coming out of timber on a rise above him, from the way he had just come.

Heart hammering, he reached for his rifle, but paused when he saw it was Horseshoe. He blinked. 'What the – what're you doing here?'

'Come to back you up,' called Horseshoe, and started the mount down the slope. 'Promised Angie I'd bring you back safe.'

Anger burned Gavin's ears. 'Dammit, I can do this! I know what to do and I don't need your help!'

'Well, you got it whether you—'

Gavin's horse jumped and almost threw him as a rifle whipcracked from a line of boulders on a ledge above where the A Bar W men were. As he fought the animal to a standstill, he watched in horror as Horseshoe was knocked out of the saddle, hit the slope awkwardly and started to slide and roll down, arms flopping limply.

Only now did the kid pull his rifle from the scab-bard, his gaze searching out the bushwhacker's posi-tion. In disbelief he watched as the man stood up, sighting down his rifle, disdaining cover so as to get in a good shot.

He was either mighty brave, or mighty stupid, Gavin thought, even as he threw himself violently out of the saddle. The bushwhacker fired and for the first time in his life, Gavin Leach found out what it was like to have a bullet driving into his flesh.

He twisted in mid-air, smashed to the ground, rifle flying from his grasp, hat gone, blood matting his pale-brown hair.

When Lindsey rode in and told Sean Rafferty he had shot both Gavin Leach and old Horseshoe, obviously mighty pleased with himself, the rancher went very still, looked back out of eyes like dark beads.

'You shot 'em *dead?*'

'I got Horseshoe in the chest, blew him clean outa the saddle, an' I got the kid in the head! His hair was all bloody and he never moved a finger after tumblin' off his hoss, chief.' Lindsey was still excited.

'*Did you go down and check?*'

Lindsey swallowed, licked his lips, didn't have to reply. Rafferty swore, clenching his fists. He glanced at Claiborne who was leaning against the wall by the door, arms folded. 'Go back with this idiot and make sure those two are dead!'

'If they're not?' Clay asked, and flinched at the whipcrack tone his boss used.

'I said *make sure they're dead!*'

Claiborne flushed. 'I savvy, chief.'

Rafferty looked worried now, toying with a pen on his desk. 'Either way, that damn drifter's going to come here looking for Lindsey – if not me! So you get back here fast, whatever you find.'

Claiborne paused as he set his hat on his head. 'Chief, he'll be after Lin, all right – so why don't we send him up into the hills for a few days?'

'What?' Lindsey asked, startled.

But the rancher nodded slowly. 'Good idea, Clay. You heard, Lin. Get some camping gear, go back to where you shot Angie's men, make sure they're dead, then head for the hills. We'll send for you when it's safe to come back.'

'Wait up! Montana'll come after me! I need some back-up if you're gonna use me as bait.' Lindsey was noticeably sweating now.

Claiborne smiled crookedly. 'You'll get your back-up, you damn fool – you just won't see me is all. Nor will Mr *Un*lucky Montana!'

The Viper River Valley was sure lush country, Montana allowed, as he made his way down the snake-like course of the river. So far he had called in at six spreads whose owners had been forced to sell to Rafferty by various means – most barely legal, some highly illegal, with terror raids or beatings and shootings.

It soon became obvious that Rafferty hadn't actually laid out much money. All the contracts were for final settlement to be made when the last ranch in the valley has been acquired by Sean Rafferty's 'Viper River Valley Development Association'.

The Irish rancher had paid at most only ten per cent of the agreed purchase price, the balance to be paid when Angie Bancroft sold Rafferty the A Bar W. It was yet another way for Rafferty to increase pressure on Angie: the other ranchers would want the rest of their money as soon as possible so would urge her to sell quickly.

Angie had said nothing to Montana about such pressure but the opportunity for it to happen was definitely there.

Most of the ranches were empty but a couple, like Asa McGovern, stayed on, waiting for the final payment, wishing they hadn't given in to Rafferty's force and signed the sale contract in the first place.

The last ranch, at the far northern end of the valley, where it began to spread out onto the plains beyond, was still inhabited by the original settlers, a middle-aged couple named Tate and Emma Pritchard. They watched Lucky approaching the house and even from twenty yards away he could see the tension in them.

He waved but it didn't relax them. The man looked solid, his clothes old and patched but clean. There was a good deal of grey in his hair although McGovern had said he was only in his mid-fifties. The woman barely came to her husband's shoulder, her colourless hair drawn back tightly, showing her pink scalp in front but doing nothing to smooth the care-worn wrinkles. There were bags under her blue eyes and she looked sad.

Montana stopped the sorrel a few yards out from the stoop which was made of packed earth rammed into a log frame, the logs notched for stability and strength like the cabin itself. Must be hard to give up a place like this, Lucky thought. *Obviously it had been built for permanence. Now. . . .*

'Howdy folks. Name's Montana. Been making the rounds of the valley and spreads bought by Rafferty.'

Tate Pritchard looked at him with his square jaw thrusting a little, silent, unsmiling. Montana gave him a minute but when he didn't reply or ask him to step down, he added, 'Maybe "bought" is the wrong word. Hate to tell you, but the way I see it, none of you are going to get any more money out of Sean Rafferty. I believe he's gonna run you out of the valley with no more than what you happen to be wearing at the time.'

Pritchard replied this time, his face colouring. 'Well, you're just the kind of visitor we been lookin' for, bringin' us good news like that!' He spat.

'Sorry, Mr Pritchard. I just wanted to get you talking. But I believe it's true. And I think you do, too.'

Emma took her husband's arm. 'We suspect it's true, but we have to hope we're wrong, Mr Montana.'

'I'd be happy for you to call me "Lucky", ma'am. I didn't come here to . . .' His words trailed off when he saw the frowns on their faces and the way Emma tightened her grip on Tate's arm. 'What's wrong?'

Tate took a deep breath. 'We heard there was someone workin' his way through the valley, checkin' out the ranches. Everyone figures you work for Rafferty.'

'Not so. You have my word I'm Angie's man.'

Tate hesitated, nodded to his wife as she said, 'Asa McGovern rode down last night. Said to watch out for a man calling himself "Lucky".'

'Well, that's me – Lucky Montana. Not necessarily a true nickname but I'm here to help in any way I can.'

111

Pritchard squinted sceptically. 'How?'

'Well, we might get round to that a little later.' Montana took a folded paper from his pocket and studied it. 'You're the last spread up this way, but there's one out on the edge of the plains, the Westmeier spread – Rafferty make them an offer, too?' As he asked, Emma went into the house and Tate said, 'Westmeier still works his place. He's just outside the valley, but he's had his troubles of late – stampedes, fences cut so his remuda wandered onto a patch of loco weed – kinda thing we all had before Rafferty turned up on the doorstep with his offer to buy.' His mouth twisted bitterly. 'On his conditions. I figure Westmeier's on his list. '

Then Emma emerged from the house holding a grubby envelope which she held up to Montana. He took it, obviously puzzled. 'Asa McGovern asked us to give this to you when you showed up. He was very nervous, wouldn't even stay for coffee, said he had to get back to Nan right away.'

Intrigued, Montana opened the envelope, swiftly read the few lines of childish words written on a piece of torn paper:

Yu best cum bak – angjie lost herd. Kid and Hossshu shot

McG

Lucky went very still, staring, reading the brief message again, taking long enough for Pritchard to ask with concern:

'Everythin' all right? Mac wouldn't tell us nothin'.'

'Worried about his wife and the baby, I guess – Rafferty's crowding Angie. Seems Gavin and Horseshoe have been shot. I'd best be going.'

As he lifted the reins, Emma said, 'Wait – your grubsack looks mighty thin. We can spare a little food.'

'Thanks, ma'am, but I'll ride straight through – be back at A Bar W by morning. Good luck.'

When Lucky Montana rode the foam-streaked horse into the Bancroft ranch yard early the next morning, Angie appeared, holding the same shotgun he had used to drive off Rafferty and Claiborne. It seemed like a long time ago now and he realized quite a deal had happened since he had shown up here.

'It's me, Angie,' he called, riding in out of the sun that was just lifting above the range like a ball of blinding white gold. She lowered the gun a little. 'I got word that Gavin and Horseshoe have been shot.'

He dismounted, loosened the cinch strap even as he spoke and she lowered the gun even more. She pushed back a stray strand of hair from her face and he saw the weariness and the deep-etched worry lines clearly.

'Horseshoe's dead,' she told him heavily. 'I don't know how Gavin managed to bring him back in his condition. . . .'

Montana mounted the porch steps. 'The kid OK?'

'He has a head wound – I think he's starting to come round now. He passed out after bringing in Horseshoe.'

He was beside her now, took her arm to steady her,

urging her back through the doorway. 'Let's see what he's got to say for himself.'

Gavin was conscious, lying in his bed in his room, but it was clear he wasn't too aware of his surroundings right now. Montana talked the woman into making a cup of coffee while he sat with Gavin, giving him time to get his bearings. He thought it best to keep Angie busy.

He sat beside the bed, touched Gavin's shoulder, and the kid's eyes fluttered half-open, a small movement in his pale gaunt face beneath the bandages swathing his head.

Speaking quietly, Lucky told him his name and that he had been head-shot and was in his own bedroom at his sister's ranch, repeating the information several times until Gavin's eyes opened all the way and stared at Montana blankly for a moment. Then he gave a wan smile.

'Howdy – Lucky. I-I went after Rafferty like a – damn fool. Got Horseshoe killed. . . .'

'No. He did the right thing riding after you, kid. You see who did the bushwhacking?'

The kid thought for a few moments, then nodded slowly. 'I saw him. So confident I wouldn't . . . give him any trouble after he shot . . . Horseshoe that he-he stood up, in the . . . open, took his time drawing his bead. . . .' He shook his head roughly, grimacing. 'Like I didn't count. I was way too slow getting my rifle out, Lucky. . . .'

'Who was it, Gavin?'

'L-Lindsey.'

Montana nodded gently, patting Gavin's shoulder.

'Just take it easy, kid. I'll handle things now. '

Gavin tried to struggle up, but it was too much. Gasping, he said, 'But it's *my* job! She's my . . . sister!'

'You proved you're game. You just got a little to learn about being trail-smart is all. Leave this with me.'

The wounded man wanted to argue, tried to hold Montana's sleeve as he stood, but his grip was way too weak. His words were slurred and trailed off before Lucky reached the bedroom door. 'Rest easy, Gav. You did good.'

In the kitchen, Angie was pouring coffe and she looked at him quizzically. 'How is he?'

'He'll be OK – just a scalp crease. Knocked him off-centre for a while. McGovern's note said something about you losing a herd?'

She nodded, brought the coffee to the table and sat down opposite him. He drank his coffee despite its scalding heat and she knew he needed something to boost his flagging energy after riding all night from the far end of the valley.

Angie told him about the stampeding of the herd into the river, the broken fence and the signs of the flash pots.

'Used them so they didn't need to shoot off their guns to stampede the herd. Gavin says it was Lindsey who bushwhacked him and Horseshoe.'

As she poured him another cup of coffee, she looked up at him. 'You're going after him, aren't you?'

He didn't answer and, genuinely puzzled, she asked, 'Why? You don't have to—' She stopped

115

abruptly and nodded gently, still watching his face. 'Of course you do! You're that kind of a man, aren't you? But it's risky, Lucky! Rafferty's obviously going all-out now to drive me off this land. He won't hesitate to order your death!'

'He likely did that long ago. But I'll nail Lindsey. That'll shake him up, make him leery about his next move.'

She frowned. 'I know you're a very hard man, Lucky, and you're used to danger, but why are you helping us? I mean, I'm more grateful than I can say for what you've done but you're a total stranger! You rode in here and—'

'I was *toted* in here, Angie – by your brother. And you doctored me.'

'Is that your answer? *The* answer? You feel you owe us something?'

'Good a reason as any.' He stood abruptly. 'I'd be obliged for a box of cartridges if you can spare some, and then I'll be on my way.'

Seeing him off on a fresh mount, a high-shouldered sorrel gelding, she said, 'Please take care, Lucky. Try to live up to your nickname, will you?'

'I'll try to *live*, Angie. That's what counts.'

She waved him off and called, 'Rafferty might've sent Lindsey away by now, knowing you'll come.'

'I'm counting on it.'

CHAPTER 10

MEANEST GUN ALIVE

Sean Rafferty was smoking, alone in his office, trying to figure his next move, when he heard men calling greetings to someone arriving in the yard.

His heart started pounding before he realized that if it was Lucky Montana no one would be shouting 'Howdy!' Annoyed with himself, he thrust back his chair, went to the window and drew the curtain aside. He frowned. Sheriff Windy Nichols was dismounting in the yard. There was a rider with him, a lanky string of a man whom Rafferty had never seen before.

The first thing he noticed was the man's height – six feet four, maybe a little more – his rawhide lean-ness, then he saw the guns.

This stranger wore two of them, in a Mexican Border *buscadero* rig, which was one wide belt with two holsters. And this one had *two* rows of cartridges. Here was a man who didn't aim to run low on ammunition. But his hips were so negligible that Rafferty wondered how they supported the weight of two heavy Colts and so many bullets.

But the man moved easily, settled the guns comfortably – Rafferty noted the holster bases were tied down to the man's thighs, though not too low – and then adjusted his hat a little, shading his eyes. His clothes were trail dusted but seemed of good quality. He followed the sheriff towards the house with long, lithe strides, looking around in a movement that seemed casual but one which the Irish rancher had seen on other men – Lucky Montana for instance.

This newcomer was a gunfighter.

He felt the tension grow as he watched the sheriff and the tall man come up onto the porch, went back thoughtfully to his desk and sat down.

When the two new arrivals came in, Rafferty was smoking easily as he toted up tally figures in the ranch ledger, glanced up casually, one finger holding down a number in his list as if it might jump off the page.

'Sheriff,' he greeted evenly, his eyes on the tall man who stood at ease, hands down at his sides, head not moving. But Rafferty knew he hadn't missed a thing.

'Howdy, Sean. Din' see Clay around. He out on the range?'

Rafferty nodded, looking directly at the tall man now. 'He's about his chores, just as you are with yours. What can I do for you? And your friend. . . .'

Nichols took the hint. 'Aw, yeah.' He turned

towards the tall man. 'Brad, like you to meet Mr Sean Rafferty, biggest man in the valley and goin' to get way bigger when he floods it and makes the desert bloom.'

Rafferty, showing his annoyance now, glared at the sheriff. Neither he nor the tall man made any move to shake hands.

'And this is . . . ?' the rancher ground between his teeth, looking steadily at the tall man now.

'Oh – Brad Dawson. He's lookin' for a man named Lucky Montana. I thought of that feller workin' for Angie Bancroft . . . I got a reply to one of my wires to a sheriff up in Wyoming, too, Sean, says there's a fugitive wanted for killin' a range detective up that way. Goes by the name of Lucky Montana. So when Brad turned up lookin' for a feller of that name, I thought of you.'

Rafferty was leery now. Was this lanky gunslinger a deputy lawman of some kind and this fool of a sheriff didn't realize it?

'Why me? He doesn't work for me,' he said carefully.

Nichols tugged at one earlobe. 'No, but I knew you had an – interest – in him. You see, Brad's a bounty hunter. An' he's chasin' down the re-ward on Lucky Montana.'

Rafferty felt a lot easier hearing that. 'I see – what I *don't* see is why you brought him here.'

'Aw, come on, Sean,' Nichols said with a wary smile. 'Brad ain't got no illusions. He heard on the way down about Montana joinin' up with Angie, which makes him your enemy.'

'Reckoned I'd get more accurate information from an enemy than one of Montana's friends,' Brad said, speaking for the first time, and in a deep, easy-on-the-ear voice, one full of confidence, and a touch of weary arrogance, too. 'I'll take him outa your hair for you, Sean.' If he noticed the stiffening of Rafferty's shoulders at the familiarity he didn't show it. 'I been chasin' this son of a bitch for more'n a year and this is the closest I've gotten to him – except for a time in Rapid City. I almost had him, but made the mistake of callin' on local law for back-up . . . made a mess of it and give him a chance to get away.'

He sounded bitter and there was a twist to his mouth, a narrowing of the cold grey eyes. Rafferty knew this man hated Lucky Montana with a passion. He figured it would be more than just the reward that was driving him.

Bounty hunters were usually cold, dispassionate men who saw their quarry not as human beings but merely as a face on a wanted dodger with a certain number of figures following a dollar sign.

But this man had a personal stake in bringing down Montana, and that suited Rafferty fine. Just in case Claiborne didn't manage to get him.

'Seems we best have a little talk – over a couple of drinks, I think.' Rafferty got to his feet and went to a cabinet where cut crystal decanters stood. As he took down glasses and poured liquor into them, he said, casually, 'I wonder if I've heard of you, Brad? What was your surname again?'

'Dawson. And if you ain't heard of me before this, you're sure gonna. And so's a lot of other people.

120

They know me up north as the "Meanest Gun Alive".'

Lucky Montana was suspicious.

He rode back to the area Gavin Leach had described as being the place where he and Horseshoe had been ambushed, and saw fresh sign around the dark-brown bloodstains.

Someone had been checking this place recently, he allowed silently, sitting back on his haunches, close to a boulder in case he needed cover quickly. He saw where Gavin had said he had seen Lindsey standing up, drawing a bead on him.

There was no one up there now, but if this was a set-up, they likely wouldn't want to kill him on Rafferty land, too – it could get sticky explaining how two of Angie's men had been shot at on Rafferty property. But he was sure they would push the unwritten law of 'trespass' that a man could shoot anyone not having legitimate business on his land.

Seemed to him, someone had come back to make sure Gavin and Horseshoe were dead. They had split here – one man riding for the hills, the other heading back to the Rafferty headquarters.

Or so the tracks showed. Plainly – *very* plainly – as if to make sure whoever came here couldn't miss them.

He figured it was Claiborne who had gone back to the ranch: he knew the tracks of the man's horse, a long-stepping grey with small feet. There was even a few silvery-grey hairs caught on the coarse surface of the boulder beside him where the horse had rubbed against it.

He glanced again up to the ridge from where Lindsey had shot Gavin Leach. The tracks that led there were larger and he knew these, too: they belonged to Lindsey's piebald.

So they had set him on the run, or he had decided to run himself when it seemed the 'dead' men weren't dead at all – not both of them, anyway.

Lucky figured Rafferty would know he would be the one to come looking, even if the kid was still alive.

He stood slowly, keeping the rifle at the ready as he looked around slowly.

'OK, gents – I'll play your game. But it'll be by my rules.'

The trail led him into the hills, going away from the river, into wild country that Rafferty claimed as part of his spread. A mighty good place for an ambush.

So he rode with rifle out, the butt resting on his thigh, hawk eyes raking the country ahead and to either side. He circled twice, cutting back across the trail, but Lindsey hadn't tried anything fancy. He was just running scared, putting as much distance between himself and Montana in the shortest possible time.

Lindsey would be scared, and rightly so: he knew he was a dead man if Montana got within gunshot range.

The heat of the day had increased considerably now and Montana was feeling it. Lack of sleep drugged him and he was not as alert as he might have been. He was aware of this and kept shaking his head occasionally, rolling a cigarette awkwardly as he kept riding. He took off his hat and poured some canteen water over his head. But he was a long way from the river up here so he used the water frugally: he didn't know when he might be able to refill the bottle.

In mid-afternoon, his horse was blowing, the sorrel's legs more used to flatter country than the steep, broken ground of these mountains. Foam slid over the dark-red glistening hide and the air snorted noisily through the flared nostrils.

Lucky knew he had to rest the animal – and himself.

He found a small brush-lined gulch not far from the top of the crest, already filled with cooling shadows. This was the place: he was impatient to get closer to Lindsey but the man had managed to hold his lead. He knew this country well and Montana figured he would need all his senses honed to a fine edge if he was to come out of this alive.

Fatigue overtook him. He punched in the crown of his hat with the bullet-holed brim, gave the horse half the water in his canteen, swigged a mouthful himself. He badly wanted a cigarette but figured the smell of tobacco would hang in the still air up here and maybe give away his position, so he settled down, hat brim over his eyes, rifle beside him under his right hand, a cartridge in the breech, thumb resting on the hammer spur.

But he fell into a deep sleep despite his resolve to only catnap, allow his weary body to recover some energy. . . .

He started awake, hammer spur going back under

his thumb, the rifle swinging up smoothly across his body so that it literally fell into his cupped left hand under the wooden forestock. But he stayed his finger on the trigger.

There was no one menacing him.

His alarm was real, though, because it was daylight and early sunshine slashed across his face as his hat fell to one side. Montana's heart was thudding against his ribs and he wasted a little breath cussing – but was glad to see the gusting steam of his words issuing from his bitter-twisted mouth. *At least it was still early, the mountains still under their usual morning chill.*

He got moving as fast as he could, chewing on jerky, knowing the horse had grazed on the succulent young brush that choked the gulch. The rifle was in his right hand as he rode out of the gulch, figuring to find some water so he could refill his canteen. There was little more than a mouthful left now. . . .

Then the rifle shot came from above and to his left, the bullet thrumming past his face. Then he was going out of the saddle, to the left, towards the gunman, because the brush was thicker there. The sorrel whinnied and plunged downslope, but only to a group of rocks which would have afforded Montana much better cover although there was too much open ground to cross first. But he rolled under the brush, poked his rifle through a gap in the branches and triggered. The bullet ricocheted some-where below the crest and he heard a man laugh.

'Thought you was s'posed to be a good shot, Montana! My old granny could do better'n that!'

124

Lucky couldn't believe it: Lindsey had been stupid enough to *come back* looking for him! He had sacrificed his lead and come looking to see if Montana was indeed following him this morning.

'You must have a death-wish, Lindsey!' Montana called, rolling to his right, and sliding back a few feet.

Lindsey had been waiting for the movement, of course, and raked the brush where Lucky had been originally. Montana heard the man swear, triggered again without aiming. Lindsey laughed again.

'Christ, I dunno why they say you're a good shot! You couldn't hit a hoss if it was standin' in front of you!'

Lindsey raked the brush again and waited. But there was no answering shot this time. The ambusher levered in another shell – and thought he heard a half-stifled moan from below. He grinned tightly, moved his position, threw the rifle to his shoulder, but held his fire.

If he climbed up to a boulder above his position he would get a better view of the brush where Montana lay – hopefully bleeding with Lindsey's bullet deep inside him. . . .

He took one last look below, saw no further movement down there, and leapt up, clambering wildly up the face of the big rock above him. It was awkward with the rifle in one hand and his body made a fine target against the light grey basalt. He reached the top, started to rise, turning, and his blood froze.

Lucky Montana was standing on the slope not ten yards away, rifle held across his body, shaking his head slowly.

'You'd be the dumbest son of a bitch I've ever met, Lindsey,' Montana said, as the Rafferty man made an effort to stand straight and get his rifle up.

Montana's Winchester blurred to his shoulder and there were two bullets in Lindsey before he unkinked his spine. His body arched and twisted as it was flung from the boulder, slid downslope, bringing a small bow wave of gravel and twigs with it. It crashed into the brush where Montana had been hiding originally and when he walked across, rifle barrel pointed at the man, hammer cocked, he knew he didn't have to put another shot into him.

He was dead and, likely, already standing in line at the gates of Hell. . . .

Lucky rode the sorrel up to the crest, found Lindsey's piebald tethered to a bush under a scraggly tree and lifted the heavy canteen from the saddle. It was nearly full and he took a long drink, gave some to the sorrel. He unsaddled the piebald and turned it loose, taking the grubsack.

He had no intention of toting Lindsey's body back: the animals could have it. But he relented enough to stack some loose rocks over it, before mounting again and turning the sorrel across the face of the mountain, figuring he wouldn't ride back the way he had come in case Claiborne or some other Rafferty man was waiting to ambush him.

It was a good enough move – but not *quite* good enough.

Claiborne rose out of the rocks behind Lucky Montana, slightly above the cowboy's trail.

'Hey! See how lucky you are this time, Montana!'

Clay couldn't resist calling, as he fired hard on the last word as Montana wrenched in the saddle, swinging his rifle up.

Too late.

Claiborne's slug slammed into him, rocking him violently in the saddle, the rifle going off but the bullet carving a path through the tree tops. He slammed across the sorrel's neck, startling it so that it whinnied and lunged away at a run, the reek of gunpowder rasping its nostrils as Lucky held on, rifle under the horse's head.

Claiborne fired several shots, bullets spurting dust, exploding bark from trees all round Montana.

He was too weak and dazed to guide the horse, feeling the crushing pain in his chest, the blood soaking his shirt and smearing across the saddle.

He knew he was hit badly – it had to be bad if it was in the chest – and wondered if his luck had finally run out as the horse plunged on across the mountain face, and the world jarred and faded in and out of focus.

One thought he had before he reached the uncaring stage, was – *How far was Claiborne behind him. . . ?*

CHAPTER 11

DEAD MAN'S EARS

Claiborne was savagely angry at himself.

Goddamnittohell! He'd had the man dead centre in his sights but that son of a bitch had lived up to his nickname, twisted a little in the saddle and instead of the bullet going squarely into his chest, it was Clay's impression that it had ripped across the front. Probably tore up the muscle and caused plenty of pain and bleeding, but that wasn't what he wanted: he wanted Montana *dead*!

Now the man had disappeared into the high timber and his damn horse had decided to play – using that frustrating, blood-pressure-lifting game of walking just beyond reach, standing still until he approached and put out a hand for the bridle, then backing-up, turning and trotting off, tail high and contemptuous, a whinny as if to say 'you can't catch me!' In no time at all he was sweating and cussing so bad that his throat was dry and raspy.

Finally – *finally* – the damn jughead had stopped

128

and allowed him to grab the bridle. Claiborne was rough with it, getting a good grip before he sheathed his rifle in the saddle scabbard and, when he climbed on board, he twisted the ears brutally, ramming home the spurs and raking viciously with the rowels. The horse, no doubt sorry it had decided to be play-ful, snorted and put on a burst of speed as Claiborne continued to rowel and jab without mercy.

Timber slowed the animal and then Claiborne had to check for tracks and blood and that slowed him even further. His mouth tightened as he examined splashes of fresh blood. Looked like the man was still mostly conscious, for he was weaving that big sorrel between the trees and brush, not plunging straight ahead and leaving a trail a blind man could follow.

But he knew if the bullet had gouged Montana's chest it would have taken out a good deal of flesh and there were plenty of blood splashes to confirm that. The man was mighty tough or riding by pure instinct. Many another man would be down by now, sprawled amongst the leaves and twigs and other forest floor detritus, moaning and bleeding, fumbling to reach his gun and having not a hope in hell of doing it before Clay would kill him.

But not this *hombre*! Tough as white cedar with a core of mountain granite. No matter! He was hit and had to be weakening by the minute – and Claiborne was on his trail and wouldn't turn back until he had the man dead. He'd take his head back to Rafferty to prove that Lucky Montana's luck had finally and irrevocably run out.

The thought cheered him up some, but he still

wanted to see that hardcase in his sights before dark this day.

Montana was still in the saddle but he didn't know for how much longer.

He had wrapped the reins around the saddlehorn and then awkwardly tied the remaining ends around his left wrist, using his teeth. The leather cut into his flesh and blood trickled over the back of his hand. He had managed to yank off his neckerchief and stuff it over the deep bullet gouge across the thick muscles of his chest, but he knew he was still bleeding plenty. The gouge was a trough, no doubt filled with bits of grit and grease from the lead missile, not to mention shreds of dirty cotton from his shirt. If loss of blood didn't kill him, it was a good bet that infection would do the job.

But these thoughts only came to him intermittently as he swayed in the saddle, the horse slowed way down by this time. They were still climbing and when they reached the crest he worked the panting animal over through timber and vegetation that was way too thin to offer much cover. He slipped almost all the way out of the saddle. Only the rein tying his wrist to the saddlehorn saved him, the pain knifing through him and waking up his brain with its messages of agony.

Straining, he fought until he was half upright, just as he topped-out on the knife edge of the mountain ridge.

A hornet buzzed wildly from a sapling over to his left and downslope a few yards. He knew what it was:

shooting upslope was always difficult and the killer had fired too low. His vision was blurred but he saw movement way back down the mountain, figuring it was Claiborne, but he didn't actually see enough detail to definitely identify the man. It would be logical though: spook Lindsey into making a run for it, holding back and allowing Montana to get behind Lindsey, even to kill the man – that way his mouth was shut permanently. Then Claiborne would come in behind Montana and finish the job.

Yeah! His chest was proof enough of what Claiborne intended. . . .

He made no attempt to shoot back now. He was too tuckered out for one thing and it was too awkward to get at his rifle in the scabbard under his left leg for another. He could easily draw his six–gun, but he would only waste lead at this distance.

Then a wave of pain and dizziness swept over him and he flopped sideways again as the rifle below hammered several shots. He heard the ricochets but none of them sounded close. Hardly knowing what he was doing, operating on pure instinct, he nudged the horse down the slope on the far side.

It seemed like a wild ride to him and yet the horse wasn't moving very fast. It, too, was weary and weakened by the long, steep climb and the constant dragging and shifting of the wounded rider's weight. It propped its forelegs on the steep incline and slid and skidded through a thin screen of brush, beginning to snort as it tried to keep control.

'Good boy! Good boy!' he slurred encouragingly. 'Ke-keep goin' . . . Keep on. . . .'

The words became unintelligible but the horse kept descending, legs quivering with the strain. Lucky's overheated brain told him that Claiborne would be coming, whipping his mount, driving it relentlessly now that he was this close. The man would be impatient to ride in for the kill.

He tried to lift his head, twist his upper body, so he could look back but the pain suddenly became a broadsword blade searching for his heart. He cried out loud and felt the horse going down under him, falling, sliding, toppling, dragging his left arm almost out of its socket. Somehow a firework exploded inside his skull and then he was nowhere that he knew because it was pitch black and there was nothing to see – or hear – or feel.

Just – nothing.

Claiborne was sweating and breathing hard by the time his horse managed to reach the crest and stumble over onto the narrow strip of flat ground before the steep slope started.

He wiped sweat out of his eyes, sitting slumped in the saddle, shoulders hunched, chin on his chest. *Goddamn but that Lucky must be tough! Up and over, then down the other side with a bullet in him and spraying blood all over the countryside. Why, Claiborne himself felt tuckered out. . . .*

He abruptly stopped his thoughts as he wiped his eyes again and saw below an unbelievable sight: Lucky Montana was down! Leastways, his horse was and the man was pinned across the still sliding sorrel, one arm somehow caught up on the saddlehorn.

132

The sorrel ploughed through bush after bush although it was slowing noticeably now, beginning to turn a little and, even as he watched, it caught up on a thicker bush and quivered to a stop. The horse struggled to get on its feet but Montana's unmoving body seemed to prevent it in some way.

Claiborne slid the rifle out of the scabbard, swung a leg over the saddle and dropped to the ground. The grey was panting and snorting and stamping about but he ignored it, stretched out behind a flat slab of shale and settled in, elbow braced, the rifle coming to his shoulder.

He concentrated on his sights, bared his teeth as he saw that Montana was still trapped and fouling the horse's efforts. Mind, the animal itself must be hurt some as well as near exhausted from the climb and the run through the timber before that.

Claiborne drew a careful bead on Montana's sprawled body. It was jerking and flopping with the movements of the horse but he could pin down the spot where the bullet would go in this time: slap-bang in the middle of that wide spread of blood across Montana's shirt front.

'So long, you son of a bitch!'

Claiborne gritted the words exultantly and his finger began to squeeze the trigger.

Then he froze as cold steel pressed into the back of his head – hatless now as he had removed it so he could sight better – and a voice he didn't know, but which sounded even colder than the touch of the gun barrel, said softly, 'Uh-uh, Claiborne – he's mine! Now you just show some good sense, lower the gun hammer, ease off the trigger, and lay the rifle down on the rock. Then turn over slowly without tryin' to get up . . . OK?' Claiborne, stiff with shock, didn't move and the gun eased up its pressure on his head – but only for a moment.

It came back in a short, sharp swing and he felt as if the back of his head had been smashed in. '*OK, I said?*'

'*Jesus!* Yeah, yeah – *OK!*'

He did as ordered, wanted to turn and look at this stranger who had come up on him from behind, his movements masked by the grey's stomping and heavy breathing, and his own fierce concentration on the rifle sights. Steel fingers gripped his shoulder, yanked him off the flat rock, and spun him onto his back.

Blinking, Claiborne stared up at the tall, lanky man holding the gun on him – and got his first good look at Brad Dawson, Meanest Gun Alive. . . .

Behind him, looking weary and worried, but hard-eyed, stood Sheriff Windy Nichols.

'Who the hell's this, Windy?' Claiborne grated.

'Sean's new trouble-shooter, Clay. Named Dawson,' the lawman answered. 'He—'

'I got an interest in Lucky Montana,' Dawson cut in, in that mellow voice. 'Now you, you get on that asthmatic jughead, ride the hell back to the ranch and check with Sean – if you gimme one little bitty piece of trouble, I got his permission to shoot the eyes outa your head – which I can, and will, do at twenty paces. You want me to try . . . ?'

'Christ, *no!*' Claiborne backed away, still sprawled,

134

watching the gun warily. 'You're – *Brad* Dawson? The bounty hunter from up north, the one they call Meanest Gun Alive?'

'In the flesh, mister. I don't see you climbin' into that saddle. . . .'

Claiborne got carefully to his feet, started to pick up his rifle, but Dawson kicked it out of reach. 'Shuck the gunbelt, too,' the bounty hunter ordered and Claiborne swallowed his protest and obeyed, looking at Nichols.

'What's goin' on, Windy?'

'Plain, enough, ain't it?' the sheriff growled. 'Dawson's Sean's top gun now – I just come along to save him from killin' you if you fussed about.'

Claiborne didn't like that but he glanced at Dawson, ran a tongue across his lips and nodded curtly. 'OK – I'll get the straight of this from the chief.'

'Aah – just get the hell outa here!' Dawson snapped, and Clay knew enough not to rile the man any further. 'Go back and relax – I'll bring you Montana's ears by supper-time.'

In two minutes Clay was back over the crest with the sheriff riding by his side, watched with narrowed eyes by Brad Dawson. The grey picked its way down the easier slope on that side, and the further he drew away, the more angry Claiborne became. He paused halfway down, looked up to where Dawson stood watching him.

But all Claiborne did was to snarl a curse and turn his horse, recklessly spurring down the mountain. Nichols followed at a good pace, anxious to get away

135

from the cold-eyed gunslinger.

Dawson watched until he could see both men riding out onto the flats and heading back up valley, before holstering his six-gun and turning to look down the slope on his side.

It appeared that Montana had come round and was trying to free his left hand from the saddlehorn. Dawson smiled and started down on foot, in sliding sideways movements, never taking his eyes off Lucky Montana who didn't seem aware of him yet.

Lucky strained to free his hand from the reins that had trapped him. The horse was still struggling to get up and if he did so, and started to run in panic – well, Montana would be in for a mighty rough ride, so he had to free himself quickly.

Then suddenly a gloved hand holding a jack knife reached from behind and slashed the reins. Montana rolled off the horse and it heaved, snorting, to its feet, cantered off a little way and stopped, watching, its ears pricked.

Montana lay there, feeling the returning blood sending stabs of lightning-like pain through his arm. He rubbed the wrist hard and looked up at his rescuer, expecting Claiborne to be there, gloating.

He stiffened when he saw Dawson and winced at pain in his chest as he tried to sit up. '*You!*'

'Yeah, Lucky – finally caught up with you after all this time.' Dawson had holstered his six-gun now and stood with boots spread a little, hands on hips, though close to his twin gun butts. 'And ain't you a *mess*! Look like you're about ready to die – are you?'

Dawson's voice was mocking and Montana stared

up at him with pain-filled eyes.

'Not . . . quite . . . yet. . . .'

Dawson grinned and stepped forward.

'Well, let's see, huh? I promised Rafferty I'd bring him your ears by supper-time – and the sun's already slidin' into the west. . . .'

It was full dark when Dawson rode back to the Rafferty spread. A quarter moon was hanging in the east, dusty red and glowing like the devil's left eye.

He wasn't surprised when Claiborne's voice called from the bunkhouse porch where the man lounged in a chair made from an empty cask padded with burlap.

'You're late, gunslinger. Couldn't be that Montana give you the slip after all, could it?'

Dawson turned from fumbling with the flap of a saddle-bag towards where he knew Claiborne to be seated, likely with other silent cowboys waiting to hear what he had to say.

He held up something dangling on a leather thong.

'These what you're worried about, Clay? Told you I'd bring back Montana's ears and here they are. Wanna close look? Or have you got a weak belly and you're afraid of losin' your supper?'

CHAPTER 12

SETTLE THE SCORE

Sean Rafferty always ate alone in his dining-room, at a polished mahogany oval table. He took his time with his meals, believing that proper digestion was necessary for a man to function properly, both physicaly and mentally.

He was dabbing at his lips after drinking the final sip of his coffee and brandy when Dawson came in unannounced and held up his trophy, dropping it onto the table amongst the empty dishes.

'That's all that's left of Mr Lucky Montana.'

Rafferty shot to his feet, his heavy padded chair toppling as the legs caught in the carpet pile. '*Get those filthy things off my table!*' he roared. '*Get them off, I said!*'

Dawson arched his eyebrows, picked up the bloody ears by the thong. 'Take it easy – they won't hurt you.'

'The hell do you mean crashing in here during my meal? Get out! We'll talk later.'

Dawson's eyes narrowed as he hooked the thong holding the wrinkled ears over the hilt of his hunting knife, keeping his deadly gaze on the rancher – who was looking decidedly less belligerent now as the gunfighter said, very quietly, 'I'm used to more courtesy than that, Sean. You want to rephrase anythin'. . . ?'

Rafferty forced himself to stay calm, flapped a hand as he righted his chair and dropped into it. 'Forgive me, Brad. Those – things – gave me a start. They're all bloody. Does that mean he was still alive when you. . . ?'

'Well, he hadn't quite started along the road to Hell. You owe me some money, I'm thinkin'. . . .'

Rafferty watched the man's hands, still too close to the gun butts for the rancher's liking. 'Of course. I can send to town for it tomorrow—'

'Or we could ride in together and get it. You pay me and then I head back north with the ears and use them to collect the bounty they got on Montana as well.'

'Ye-es – but I've just had another idea, Brad. Sit down.'

Dawson made himself comfortable. 'What's this big idea you've got?'

'You don't give a damn for a man's – standing, do you?' Rafferty couldn't hide his annoyance.

'You mean "my betters"? Hell, far as I'm concerned I ain't yet met a man I consider is better'n me, Sean. Present company included.'

Rafferty's face flushed and he snapped, 'Don't be impertinent!'

Dawson sighed and started to get up. 'Look, you gonna tell me your idea or you gonna give me a lesson in manners? I'm damn hungry and I'm tired.'

Rafferty quickly held up a placating hand, forced a crooked smile. 'I won't waste any more of your time, Brad, I promise.' Dawson sat again, waiting impatiently. 'I was thinking – seeing as you've killed Montana and Horseshoe's dead and Angie's kid brother is laid up wounded—'

'How you know that?'

'I've had a man watching her place. Anyway, considering those things and that I am being pressured hard by my backers to finish the acquisition of land in the valley' – he paused, spread his hands – 'well, now would seem a good time to force the issue, *make* Angie Bancroft sign the sale contract.'

Dawson appeared just as casual and relaxed as earlier but there was a growing spark of interest in his bleak eyes. 'These fellers you got waitin' in the wings – your backers – they gonna give you money soon as you sign up this Bancroft woman? I mean *give* you money, not just promise it?'

Rafferty hesitated, more watchful now, but he nodded slowly. 'Yes. I need working capital so I can show my good faith to the Lands Commissioner and then—'

'Then he'll put up *his* cash, or make it available to you . . . right?'

'That's right.' Rafferty spoke a little slower now,

carefully studying this gunfighter. 'You seem to know something about this kind of thing, Brad?'

Dawson shrugged. 'Wasn't always a gunfighter and bounty hunter – worked for a big lumber company in Oregon once. I was a foreman and the company got into trouble, needed investors and got a little gov'ment money to help 'em out buildin' a string of new army forts. But the company directors split the gov'ment money and lit out for parts unknown. Was my first bounty-huntin' chore, bringin' 'em in. . . .'

He let the rest drift off but it appeared to satisfy Rafferty although he seemed much more wary now.

'That your idea?' Dawson asked softly. 'Let some of that gov'ment money stick to your fingers?'

Rafferty stood slowly. 'Shall we get Claiborne and go see Angie right now?'

Dawson stood. 'How about we leave it till mornin'? I need to get on the outside of some supper first.' He paused behind his chair, looking down at Rafferty. 'Might be an idea if you took that slimy sheriff along. His signature as a witness could help show it's all above board and bind the contract a little tighter.'

'Yes, that's fine. Windy is staying here overnight. He and Clay didn't get in till just before dark – fortuitous, eh?'

Dawson went out and Rafferty sat back, lips pursed, drumming thick fingers on the edge of the table.

That gunslinger wasn't as dumb as he looked. . . .

*

The man Rafferty had had watching the Bancroft place was called Bo Clanton and he was yawning, just waking up when he heard the riders coming down the slope of the hogback rise where he had been all night. *He hadn't expected anyone this early.* Then he recognized Rafferty in the lead, followed by that new gunslinger Dawson, Claiborne and Windy Nichols bringing up the rear

Bo felt guilty because he had slept past sun-up, so before Rafferty could throw a question at him he said, 'Everythin's hunky-dory, Mr Rafferty. No visitors durin' the night.'

He hadn't even been awake long enough to study the ranch yard beyond the rise, but Rafferty didn't seem aware of this. 'Then there's still only Angie and the kid there?' he asked.

Bo nodded enthusiastically. 'That's the way it is, Mr Rafferty.'

'All right, Bo, you can go on back to the ranch and have a decent breakfast.'

Bo Clanton's hunger was more or less legendary on every ranch he had ever worked and he departed quickly, eager to front-up to the breakfast table and a heaping pile of greasy food.

By then, Claiborne, belly down at the crest, was focusing his field-glasses on the house below.

'Smoke comin' outa the kitchen chimney,' he reported, sweeping the lenses around slowly. 'No extra hosses I can make out. Montana's sorrel ain't there, leastways—'

'Were you expecting it?' Rafferty asked curtly and Clay shrugged, looking hard at Dawson.

142

'Just checkin' – them ears could belong to anybody.'

Dawson stepped forward and kicked Claiborne hard in the ribs. The man gasped, grabbed at his side, rolling over, face contorted. He fumbled for his six-gun but Dawson's boot pinned the hand to his body. The gunfighter shook his head.

'Don't be a bigger fool than you already are, Clay.' he said easily. 'You're lucky I don't kill you. . . .'

'Please leave it until after we have Angie's name on the bill of sale,' Rafferty said tiredly, glaring at both men. 'If you are both ready, gentlemen . . . ?'

Sheriff Windy Nichols ran a tongue over his lips, plainly wanting no part of this, but not game enough to say so.

Riding in a tight group, they crested the hogback and rode down into the yard.

By the time they were dismounting at the corrals, Angie Bancroft stood on the porch, holding the long-barrelled Greener as if she knew what she was doing – which she did.

'*Far enough!*' she called, her voice steady, lifting the gun and pointing it in their direction.

Immediately, Claiborne grinned and started moving away from the others, towards the right-hand corner of the house. Angie looked bothered, trying to make a quick decision: where did she aim the gun now? At Claiborne – or the others? Then Nichols, at a word from Rafferty, began to edge towards the left-hand corner of the house.

'Stop!' Angie cried, lifting the gun as she thumbed back the hammers with audible clicks.

143

Nichols froze but Claiborne laughed and kept moving.

'You pull the triggers, Angie, and you shoot off both barrels, you'll maybe get Windy *or* me, but only one of us – and you'll still have three to face. Why don't you show good sense and put down the Greener and listen to what Mr Rafferty has to say?'

As he was speaking he kept moving and on his last words he took three long steps and disappeared around the house corner. When Angie snapped her head back the other way, she was just in time to see Windy Nichols' lower leg as he jumped out of sight around the left-hand corner.

When she swung back, she cried out in alarm: Brad Dawson was standing almost on top of her, reaching for the shotgun, forcing her hand away from the hammers, as he twisted the weapon from her grip.

'There now, lady, ain't that better? No decisions to make, no gun to kick you in the belly or the chest. Just you, and Mr Rafferty's proposition. . . .'

As he wrenched the gun from her grip with one hand, he grabbed one of her arms with the other, led her to the top of the steps and moved away, unloading the Greener. He tossed the gun in one direction and the two shells in another.

Angie, white-faced, breathing hard, faced Rafferty now, Claiborne and Nichols coming back from around the sides of the house. 'What d'you want?' she demanded. 'You've killed Horseshoe and my brother's worsening by the minute . . . Montana never returned so I assume you killed him, too?'

144

'Forget Montana – his luck's run right out.' Dawson grinned and indicated the ears on their thong, dangling from his bone knife handle.

She grimaced and looked at him coldly. 'Lucky said you were a cold-blooded murderer!'

Dawson bowed slightly. 'He musta been feelin' good – usually he calls me a lot worse'n that.' He grabbed her arm and, as she struggled, he spoke to Rafferty. 'You ready, Sean?'

'Yes – let's do this in comfort,' Rafferty smiled, in a good mood now. He started up the steps, and chuckled as Dawson dragged Angie through the door into the parlour.

'You keep watch outside, Clay,' the Irishman said over his shoulder and, as Windy Nichols followed the others inside, Claiborne scowled and dropped into one of the split-cane chairs on the porch, reaching for his tobacco sack.

He felt left out of things – something that was happening more and more since the arrival of that son of a bitch Dawson. . . .

Then he jumped at the crash of a gunshot inside, leapt up and went through the door with his six-gun in his hand, but there was no trouble. It seemed that Gavin Leach had been propped up with cushions on the sofa, bandages around his head, and he had dragged a pistol out from somewhere and taken a shot at either Rafferty or Dawson.

Too bad he missed! Then Dawson slapped him across the face, tore the Colt from his grip with his other hand. The bounty-hunter glanced at Claiborne.

'Nice fast move, Clay, but everythin's under

control. Go finish your doze on the porch.'

Claiborne scowled and went outside, his jaw jutting like Bison Butte above the whitewater rapids at the bend of the river. . . .

Angie pulled free of Nichols' grip on her arm and knelt swiftly beside Gavin. One side of his face was reddened, white finger-shapes showing through the patch of colour. 'Are you all right, Gav?'

'Sure, Sis.' The young wounded man glared at Dawson who had a mocking look on his face, totally unconcerned. 'Take more than a slap from that killer to put me off my grub!'

Dawson grunted, 'I'd say she's all yours now, Sean.'

'Sit down at the table, please, Angie,' Rafferty requested and, when she tilted her jaw at him defiantly, he merely nodded slightly to Dawson who dragged her to the small table, pulled out a straight-back chair and sat her down on it roughly.

'Take it easy, damn you!' Gavin said, thrusting up onto his elbow but going pale with the effort.

Rafferty spread a sheaf of papers in front of Angie and Windy Nichols brought over an ink bottle and nib pen from the small writing bureau in the corner, setting them near her right hand. The rancher flicked through the three or four pages of closely written words.

'I'm sure you would be bored with all the legalese, Angie, so I'll explain it to you simply: this is a contract for sale of your land and its goods and chattels to myself—'

'Then you might as well throw it into the kitchen stove,' she told him defiantly. 'I have no intention of signing any such document.'

Dawson winked at Gavin and next instant he was standing behind the wounded man, holding his hair brutally, dislodging the bandage, revealing part of the head wound, almost pulling the hair strands out of the kid's scalp. His hunting knife blade rested casually against Gavin's left ear.

Angie paled and her eyes went involuntarily to the ears dangling on the leather thong on Dawson's belt. 'No!' she cried.

Rafferty smiled like a hungry snake suddenly finding food and offered her the pen, handle first, the nib already loaded with ink. 'Just beside your printed name on the last page, if you will, Angie, my dear. I will date it later, so you won't be inconvenienced . . . Hmm?'

Angie made no move to take the pen, looked at Gavin now. He was still writhing, but not so violently, as his hair was held taut and his scalp felt as if it was tearing away from his skull. Sweat sheened his gaunt face. 'Sis . . . don't . . . do . . . it!'

'It's all the same to me, kid. Been wantin' to try and slice off an ear with just one stroke but they always struggle and make me saw away. You any idea how tough that cartilage is?'

'*Stop it!*' Angie croaked, looking sick. 'What kind of a monster are you?'

Dawson shrugged. 'Aw, I dunno – just your average bloody-handed fiend, I guess. Nothin' fancy. . . .'

'Sis! Don't sign it!'

'You notice how his voice begins to sound like a woman's?' Dawson said, smiling. 'How about we try for soprano?'

Angie desperately swung towards Rafferty. 'Stop him, can't you?'

'*You're* the one who can stop him, my dear,' the Irishman said with a smiling smirk, as he thrust the pen towards her. 'Perhaps just a small nick to start with, Brad?'

'Sis!' Gavin tried to wrench his head aside and she snatched the pen quickly and scrawled her signature where Rafferty indicated, slumping in her chair.

'Aw, hell!' Dawson said, obviously disappointed. He thrust Gavin's face roughly into the pile of cushions and the kid rubbed hard at his stinging scalp, a thin trickle of blood crawling down his face. 'Shouldn't've done it, Sis!'

'I had to! You know I had to!' She glared at Rafferty, shaking. 'Well, you have everything now – I suppose you're going to throw me off my land right away?'

'Oh, I'm not a hard man, despite what you may think, Angie. I have no objection to you nursing your young brother back to health before moving out. I'll extend you the same courtesy as I did the others in the valley: you can wait until my money comes through from the government.'

'I signed a bill of sale for A-Bar-W and I want the full purchase price within twenty-four hours!'

'Ah, but see, you didn't take time to read the fine print, my dear. Ten per cent downpayment, it says. You agreed to wait for the other ninety per cent until after I am paid the government subsidy. Oh, Sheriff Nichols, would you be good enough to witness my signature?'

'Sure thing, Sean.'

The two men bent over the paper, signing their names, while Angie stood trembling, hands clasped in front of her, face bloodless.

'It's too late to worry now, Sis,' Gavin said quietly. 'There's nothing anyone can do now you've signed.'

'Aw, I dunno – I reckon this can be sorted out easily enough.'

They all looked up quickly – for it had been Brad Dawson who had spoken.

Something in his tone chilled Rafferty although Dawson's guns were still holstered and his knife had been returned to its sheath.

'What the devil's this?' the Irishman hissed and Nichols, frowning, out of his depth with this sudden switch, started to edge towards the door.

'Wait up there, Sheriff. Like a word with you. And with Mr Rafferty. Ma'am, if you'd move a'ways to your left. . . .'

A trifle dazed, Angie, moved as ordered. Dawson's eyes were on the sheriff and Rafferty – both men were tensed, wary, trying to figure things out. Dawson winked at both men and Gavin held his breath, glancing at his sister who seemed in shock.

'You wanna join us now, *amigo*?'

They stiffened as Dawson raised his voice and then Lucky Montana, looking trail stained and weary, moving stiffly, appeared in the hall doorway, coming through from the back of the house, a bandage showing at the neck of his torn, bloodstained shirt. He had a cocked six–gun in his right hand. Angie gasped.

'I don't believe in ghosts,' she said slowly, 'so. . . .'

Lucky seemed grateful to be able to lean a shoulder against the door jamb. He smiled crookedly at Rafferty. 'Still got both ears, Sean – see?'

Rafferty's face enpurpled and his eyes narrowed, veins stood out in his throat and on his forehead as he swivelled his hate-filled gaze at Dawson. 'You double-crossing son of a bitch!'

Brad Dawson laughed. 'Hey, figured an Irishman from the peat bogs could come up with somethin' a bit more colourful than that, Sean.'

Rafferty was shaking now. 'No bogs, damn you! I was only eight years old when I came here. I've been away far too long, but I've never forgotten those emerald green fields on the old estate.'

'Might've been better if you had, Sean,' Dawson told him quietly. 'Bit of a wild dream you had about reclaimin' the family estate after all these years, wasn't it?'

Rafferty's head jerked, jaw thrusting. 'What d'you know about it?'

'A lot more than you want me to, Sean.' Rafferty obviously didn't understand, looking from the silent Montana back to Dawson and the latter said, 'Had a lot of complaints from folk in the valley about the way you were buyin' 'em out. Small deposit and keepin' 'em waitin' with no real guarantee you were gonna pay up.'

'I resent that! I fully intended—'

'No you didn't,' Dawson cut in coldly, and Rafferty subsided at his tone, sensing he was close to big trouble here. 'There were too many complaints so we took a much closer look at you then, Sean. Learned about how your stepmother had cheated you out of a share in the family estate and then, through drink and scheming lovers, lost whatever money was left and allowed it all to fall into ruin.'

'Yes, the bitch!' Rafferty gritted, unable to hold back his hatred for the old woman far across the seas. 'That's why I worked so hard to get the money to buy it back, but – I had only enough for the deposit. . . .'

'But it left you mighty short of cash, after you sent the money over to Ireland, agreein' to find the rest by a certain date.'

Rafferty seemed calmer now, cold, in fact, accepting that his deception had been discovered. But his eyes were murderous.

'Which is why you could only afford to pay the ranchers a small deposit. You needed their land because the gov'ment won't put in any money to your scheme until you have it. And when they do, Sean, you'll be on the next ship out of New York with all those thousands, headed for County Antrim . . . right?'

'That was my plan, yes,' Rafferty said heavily. 'And I'd like to know how you know so much about it!'

'Well, it's finished now, Rafferty,' said Montana, drawing all eyes. 'The whole deal's in ruins, just like your mouldy old castle.'

Before Montana could say any more, Windy Nichols, ever ready to cover his own back, asked, 'Who are you fellers, anyway? You sure ain't talkin' like any gunslinger or outlaw I know.'

Everyone in the room was hanging on the reply and Dawson glanced at Montana, then said, 'Speakin' for myself, I'm a Special Investigator for the Federal Lands Commissioner. I kind of deputized Lucky here, caught up with him just before Murphy Creek, and figured I could use a man like him, good with a gun, quick-thinkin' – so I put it to him: help me nail this Irish son of a bitch who's trying to steal gov'ment money and I'd see that they took away all them wanted dodgers out on him. That, or I took him in and he could stare ten, twelve years in jail right in the face. 'Course that damn fool of a range detective who tried to claim a bounty on him almost wrecked things, but Lucky knows which side his bread's buttered. He kept his part of the bargain when the kid there rescued him from the desert – so I reckoned it was up to me to keep my part – and here we are . . . just needed to actually witness one of your slimy deals, Sean – and this was the big one, wasn't it? Get Angie's place and you could put in your claim to the Lands Commissioner.'

The look on Rafferty's face should have killed both men where they stood but there was fear mixed with the hatred, too. He said, angrily, 'I have a letter from the commissioner himself advising me he is willing to sink many hundreds of thousands of dollars into my scheme. He recognizes it as a project worthy of government support, one that will be of benefit to everyone, a public-spirited plan to take this state forward into the next century. And, by a happy coincidence this happens to be the commissioner's home state.'

'You sound like a politician, Sean. Havin' been born here is why he wanted to make *damn* sure everything's well and truly above board. Very damn sure!' Dawson said flatly, and it clearly shook Rafferty.

'Not such a "happy coincidence" after all, eh, Rafferty?' Montana said. 'That was one thing to upset your plans – and then there was me.'

'But you – you're an outlaw!' said Angie suddenly. 'By your own admission!' She glanced at Dawson. 'And you said this bounty-hunter was pursuing you and wouldn't give up!'

'All true, Angie. When Dawson finally ran me down and put his deal to me, I had no choice. I'd been on the run for too long. I was glad to make any deal to get the bounty off my head.'

'I don't understand,' Angie said. 'You were really near death in the desert when Gavin found you – that wasn't faked.'

'Damn right it wasn't. It was only pure chance that the river we jumped into joined the Viper and carried me this way – I figured it was a sign, maybe a change of luck. The original idea was for me to work for Rafferty: thought he wouldn't be suspicious of anyone with so many wanted dodgers out on him.'

Rafferty stirred, very tense now, his eyes the colour of mud. But he remained silent.

'But after Gav took me to Angie's I reckoned it'd be better if I worked for her, seeing as she was one of

Rafferty's enemies; that way he wouldn't figure I was investigating him. But you were still suspicious, weren't you, Sean?'

'With that much money at stake? I wasn't going to take anything at face value. I admit you had me fooled, Montana: I thought you really were just a killer on the run.' His face abruptly crumpled and his voice trembled, choking with his emotion. '*Damn* you! You and this – this cadaverous gunslinger have ruined my plans! All I wanted was to regain my family's honour, show those smug brothers of mine that I could make our estate in Ireland flourish again; I was the one who could give the Rafferty name back the respect it deserves! I – I. . . .'

'Well, chief, sounds to me like this is as good a time as any to get rid of these interferin' bastards.'

The words were hurled into the room by Claiborne in the porch doorway, eyes hard and murderous, legs planted firmly, six-gun in hand. He swung the weapon onto Dawson first and let the hammer slip from under his thumb, baring his teeth in satisfaction. But the look turned to one of shock – and pain – as Dawson's twin guns came up flaming before Claiborne's hammer fell.

Three bullets smashed into him, the impact driving him back to the rail where his hips struck, somersaulting him over to fall flat on his face in the yard.

By then, Lucky Montana's Colt was blazing and Windy Nichols cried out as a bullet shattered his elbow. The sheriff fell to his knees, dropping his gun, screaming in pain. Rafferty dived for the door, gun out, shooting wildly.

One shot struck Nichols and knocked him flat. Dawson lunged after the rancher but stopped as if he had run into a tree suddenly growing in the doorway. He spun and went down, clutching at his side. Stumbling a little, Montana stepped forward and shot over Dawson's head. He brought down Rafferty in a cloud of dust, the big Irishman twisting to fire back – and keep firing until his gun was empty. Or until Montana's next bullet slammed the life out of him – it never was clear which.

Splinters flew from the doorway all around Montana but none touched him before Rafferty fell back and died, coughing red blood down his shirt front.

When he turned back into the room, Lucky saw Angie working over Dawson who was slumped against a wall, his open shirt revealing a bloody hole in his side.

Montana looked as he reloaded his gun. 'Your land's safe now, Angie.'

Her eyes were moist as she raised them to Lucky's gaunt face. 'Thanks to you two.'

'Say,' asked Gavin, managing to rise to a half-sitting position as he addressed Dawson. 'Whose ears were they, anyway?'

'Lindsey's. He din' have no more use for 'em.'

Angie shuddered slightly. 'What're you two going to do now? Your job's finished, isn't it?'

Dawson and Montana exchanged glances.

'Well, Rafferty's took care of,' Dawson said slowly,

pushing Angie aside suddenly so that she gave a small cry as she fell against the wall. He struggled up, grimacing, bloody, one gun down at his side in his right hand. He was looking at Montana. 'Lucky, you could've just rid out after Angie doctored you when the kid brought you in from the desert. But you never . . . why?'

Montana was tense now. 'We had a deal.'

Dawson smiled and shook his head slowly. 'Knew it! I'd trailed you for a year and all that time I told myself *Hell, this feller's tough as they come but he's got one weakness.* Know what it is, Lucky? *Honour!* You're a goddamned man of honour!'

'Some might see it as a weakness – I don't.'

'No – well, I do. And I've never been honourable. Thanks for your help, *amigo*, but you still got some big bounties on you.'

'You – you promised to get them removed!' Angie said, shocked. 'You gave Lucky your word!'

'Like I said, never was much on this 'code' thing.' His gun started to lift. 'Sorry, *amigo*, we could make a good partnership but you'd foul-up tryin' for fair play. Me? I'll take the cash in hand.'

Both guns crashed together and Angie screamed, throwing herself aside. Dawson slammed back against the wall, his eyes wide open in shock – or pain. He half-turned, his gun firing again into the floor. Then he collapsed, silently.

Lucky looked down at him, lowered his gun hammer.

'Well, he might've been the *meanest* gun alive,' observed Gavin slowly, 'but he sure wasn't the *fastest*!'

Montana helped the shaking Angie to her feet. She looked up into his face. 'You'll have to ride out now.'

He nodded. 'Kinda used to it.'

'Will you come back sometime? When you feel it's safe. . . ?

He smiled slowly. 'Why not? A man never knows his luck.'